theatre & empire

theatre & empire

Benjamin Poore

 palgrave

First published 2016 by
PALGRAVE

Palgrave in the UK is an imprint of Macmillan Publishers Limited,
registered in England, company number 785998, of 4 Crinan Street,
London, N1 9XW.

Palgrave Macmillan in the US is a division of St Martin's Press LLC,
175 Fifth Avenue, New York, NY 10010.

Palgrave is a global imprint of the above companies and is represented
throughout the world.

Palgrave® and Macmillan® are registered trademarks in the United States,
the United Kingdom, Europe and other countries.

ISBN 978–1–137–44306–9 paperback

This book is printed on paper suitable for recycling and made from fully
managed and sustained forest sources. Logging, pulping and manufacturing
processes are expected to conform to the environmental regulations of the
country of origin.

A catalogue record for this book is available from the British Library.

A catalog record for this book is available from the Library of Congress.

Printed in China

contents

series editors' preface

The theatre is everywhere, from entertainment districts to the fringes, from the rituals of government to the ceremony of the courtroom, from the spectacle of the sporting arena to the theatres of war. Across these many forms stretches a theatrical continuum through which cultures both assert and question themselves.

Theatre has been around for thousands of years, and the ways we study it have changed decisively. It's no longer enough to limit our attention to the canon of Western dramatic literature. Theatre has taken its place within a broad spectrum of performance, connecting it with the wider forces of ritual and revolt that thread through so many spheres of human culture. In turn, this has helped make connections across disciplines; over the past 50 years, theatre and performance have been deployed as key metaphors and practices with which to rethink gender, economics, war, language, the fine arts, culture and one's sense of self.

Theatre & is a long series of short books which hopes to capture the restless interdisciplinary energy of theatre and performance. Each book explores connections between theatre and some aspect of the wider world, asking how the theatre might illuminate the world and how the world might illuminate the theatre. Each book is written by a leading theatre scholar and represents the cutting edge of critical thinking in the discipline.

We have been mindful, however, that the philosophical and theoretical complexity of much contemporary academic writing can act as a barrier to a wider readership. A key aim for these books is that they should all be readable in one sitting by anyone with a curiosity about the subject. The books are challenging, pugnacious, visionary sometimes and, above all, clear. We hope you enjoy them.

Jen Harvie and Dan Rebellato

theatre & empire

The Empire of Empires

The historical age of empires may be over, but empire as an idea continues to exercise a hold on our imaginations. On our screens, expansive long-form dramas like the *Star Wars* franchise or *Game of Thrones* populate their fictional universes with empires, warring dynasties and imperial rebels. The word 'empire' and its related terms (imperial, colonial) have broadened their meaning in political discourse and popular culture to encompass anything a speaker may dislike or disapprove of. As Stephen Howe observes, '"Imperialism", as a word, has gone imperial; "colonialism" has colonised our languages' (l. 407). The only example I've found where that's not the case is in entrepreneurship, where being the founder of a 'business empire', like Alan Sugar or Donald Trump, is noted as an admirable achievement and one to be emulated. Given the route through the subject of theatre and empire that I intend to navigate in this book, I find this to be a telling exception.

In politics, successive British prime ministers since the 1990s have had difficulty finding a plausible, consistent way to talk about the UK's imperial past. Most egregiously, Labour Prime Minister Tony Blair's premiership was bookended by his apologizing for the sins of the British Empire. Blair apologized on Britain's behalf for the Irish famine in 1997, and issued a statement of 'deep sorrow and regret' about British involvement in the slave trade in 2007. But the years in between those dates were marked by a remarkably comprehensive set of decidedly neo-imperialist aims and interventions (Ferguson, p. 375). Of course, the interventions under Blair's government that still resonate in domestic and global politics, as I write this, are the invasions of Afghanistan in 2001 and Iraq in 2003 as part of an international coalition led by the United States of America. This book sets out to argue that the UK's support of what US President George W. Bush called the 'war on terror' has galvanized British playwrights, directors and companies during the last two decades. As we'll see, it has led to a wide range of plays that make implicit and explicit comparisons between US imperialism and the empires of the past.

The question of whether American global hegemony *can* be interpreted or named as an 'empire' has generated heated debate since the fall of the Berlin Wall in 1989 and increasingly so in the wake of the Afghanistan and Iraq occupations (Immerman, ll. 143–63). For its opponents, the 'invisible empire' of the United States is imperialism carried into the twenty-first century and is all the more sinister because it exercises power by unseen routes. President Bush may have insisted in 1999 that 'America has never been an empire' (l. 117), but the much-quoted comment of the anonymous senior adviser to Bush in 2004 – 'We're an empire now, and when we act, we create our own reality' – confirmed, for many others, the nature of the United States' self-regard and its true purpose (quoted in Chomsky, p. 10). Hence, in the theatre, a play like David Greig's *The American Pilot* (The Other Place, RSC, 2005) can have its titular character crash-land in the hills of an unnamed, Middle Eastern country, and the situation – its political, military and cultural tensions – can be enough to maintain audience interest by playing on the familiar and the unexpected elements of such a generic encounter. And in the recent plays of David Hare, *Stuff Happens* (Olivier, National Theatre, 2004) and *The Vertical Hour* (Music Box Theatre, New York 2006, and Royal Court, London 2008), American empire is mentioned, in passing, almost as a given in the former (pp. 9, 33) or in the latter, as an overfamiliar conceit that's nevertheless proved true by experience (p. 51).

At the same time, the deployment of British armed forces abroad and comparisons with American military might have forced a sharpened awareness of the UK's post-imperial stature. A flood of new histories of the British Empire have attempted to reassess it and the lessons it may hold for 'those aware of the ramifications of global imperialism in the contemporary moment' (Burton, p. 275). Yet the general consensus that empires are bad things doesn't seem to have made agreement about the British Empire and its legacy any easier for historians. Niall Ferguson argues that 'no organisation in history has done more to promote the free movement of goods, capital and labour than the British Empire', and credits it as the foundation of global trade (p. 12). But he also defends the British Empire's moral character, suggesting that being ruled by the British was preferable to the 'far more oppressive empires' of the twentieth century (p. 298). By contrast, Richard Gott rejects such notions as the 'rose-tinted spectacles of heritage culture' and asserts that 'Britain's imperial experience ranks more closely with the exploits of Genghiz Khan or Attila the Hun than with those of Alexander the Great' (p. 3). Philippa Levine likewise asserts that 'the British Empire was not a benign and kindly force when compared with its rivals, but a powerhouse always capable of attempting to impose its will through violence and coercion' (l. 141). John Darwin, on the other hand, concurs with Ferguson's relativist position ('the imperial frying-pan was not the worst place to be') in *The Empire Project* (l. 345). Similarly, Kathryn Tidrick insists that 'Empires happen, have always happened, and need not be singled out for special feelings of contrition' (p. xii).

So, why this book? What makes thinking about theatre, theatre history, empire and the history of empires important and productive now? Well, firstly, the combined interest in the British Empire that was and the US empire that (arguably) is has led to an upsurge of plays on imperial themes in British theatre. These have often been staged at high-profile venues like the Royal Court, the RSC and the

National Theatre. In number and variety, these recent plays on empire easily outstrip the cycle of British Empire plays of the 1960s and 1970s, which were staged when decolonization was still a recent memory (Poore, p. 47). Why should this be so?

One possibility is that the haste with which decolonization was achieved in the 1950s and 1960s (Ferguson, pp. 256–7; Rebellato, pp. 135–6) has left a prevailing sense that the loss of empire is 'unfinished business', something that mainstream British culture has been avoiding, but whose moral, military and economic consequences Britain must come to terms with sooner or later. David Edgar's *Destiny* (RSC, 1977) implies one such reckoning, as the play follows a group of soldiers, officers, administrators and servants from the British withdrawal from India in 1947. Each character eventually settles in the West Midlands town of Tattley and becomes involved in political debates over immigration and trade union discrimination against Asian workers, which imply that imperial attitudes of racial superiority have never really gone away. Again, it's at moments of national crisis – like the Enoch Powell 'rivers of blood' controversy on which the incidents of *Destiny* are evidently based, or in times of war, like the Falklands and Afghanistan and Iraq – that these underground streams of (in varying quantities, for different sections of the population) confusion, bitterness, nostalgia and guilt seem to emerge in post-imperial drama. As Emma Cox has pointed out in her contribution to this series, *Theatre & Migration,* the traditional flows of white people to the outposts of empire have been reversed in the last fifty years (pp. 57–60), and how we deal with the attempts of large numbers of people to make their way to Europe, partly as a result of the world that European imperialism created, is one of the pressing political and ethical – and theatrical – subjects of today.

Secondly, there is a genealogy of British plays about empire in the post-decolonization period that has not yet been traced. While academic research has given us a strong set of reference points, examples and patterns to enable us to discuss the representation of empire on the nineteenth-century stage, there's little equivalent scholarship on modern plays about imperial history – apart from the crucial but necessarily disparate work of postcolonial theatre studies. Plays featuring imperial conflicts have been some of the most discussed and admired theatrical events of the last half century, from *The Romans in Britain* (Olivier, National Theatre, 1980) to *Black Watch* (Edinburgh Festival Fringe, 2006). Plays about empires have also consistently made it onto English Literature and Drama syllabuses as set texts, including John Arden's *Serjeant Musgrave's Dance*, Peter Shaffer's *The Royal Hunt of the Sun*, Caryl Churchill's *Cloud Nine*, Timberlake Wertenbaker's *Our Country's Good* and Brian Friel's *Translations*. In obtaining exam text status, these plays have helped to form the ideas successive generations have about what theatre is and can be, although many of them have not been discussed as empire plays but as history plays or 'anti-war' plays instead. Critical consideration of modern empire plays, as a group or a tradition, has been scant. This book takes a small step towards describing such a field in the British context.

Theatre & Empire does not, however, focus on the field of postcolonial drama. No book of this length could hope to do justice to such 'exceptionally varied theoretical and thematic territory' (Balme, p. vii), and it would run the risk, through omission and simplification, of overgeneralizing about 'the postcolonial condition' or 'the postcolonial subject', which varies enormously depending on the nature of a country or region's interaction with imperial powers, and which ones, and in which order (Loomba, p. 36). Instead, this book will address the 'theatre of empire' that has been produced over roughly the last fifty years, with a particular focus on theatre since the new millennium. In this modern theatre of empire, playwrights and companies have presented accounts of how empires work, as political, military, economic and cultural entities. As a scholar of British theatre history, I will concentrate primarily on Anglophone theatre produced or performed in the UK, but I want to draw on comparisons with theatre from, and depicting, other empires, especially the Roman Empire. As I'll show, the Roman world – not just the period of the emperors but from the late Republic onwards – has served as a constant point of comparison for all modern empires.

The outlook of *Theatre & Empire* is not intended to imply that British theatre somehow has a monopoly on reflecting on the bombast, pageantry, fear, violence, greed and shame of empire – far from it. Still less is it an argument for special pleading, a querulous insistence that 'the imperialists suffered too' or that there was 'bad on both sides'. On the contrary, as I'll show, theatre of empire has thrived in the UK over the last two decades because it has emphasized untold stories of empires and adopted neglected perspectives. This book is born of a belief that the theatre is one of the few places where sustained reflection is possible on what an empire is – and inevitably, whether we're still caught in an imperial moment today, as subjects within the empire of empires.

The structure of the rest of the book is as follows. In the first part of the book, I'll explore the parameters of theatre and empire. I'll begin with a case study of Third World Bunfight's *Exhibit B* in order to explore some of the challenges of representing imperialism for modern audiences. I'll then offer some simple, workable definitions of empire, and pick my way through some of the many, often contradictory, theories of empire in the modern age. After that, the book suggests a range of ways that we might think about theatre and empire, empire and theatre, and empire *as* theatre – a kind of rehearsal and a kind of performance. In the second part of the book, I use cultural imperialism and economic imperialism as different yet complementary frameworks for exploring theatre's recent engagements with empire. In the third part, I suggest three types of empire plays that can be identified by looking across from recent productions to some of the classic plays of the late twentieth century. Finally, I interpret these play types in the light of the theories of empire discussed in part one.

The Human Zoo

In September 2014, the artist Brett Bailey's work *Exhibit B* was due to be shown at the Vaults in London, under the auspices of the Barbican Centre. As it had received a positive review from Lyn Gardner of *The Guardian* while it was being staged at the Edinburgh Festival the previous month, London audiences were anticipating a discomfiting experience that served as a reminder that 'Britain's 21st-century ways of seeing are still strongly skewed by ... colonial attitudes' (Gardner, 'Exhibit B – facing the appalling reality of Europe's colonial past'). In the event, *Exhibit B* was cancelled by the Barbican after protests outside the venue, and a reported attempt to force the doors, led to the decision that it would be unsafe to proceed.

It's understandable that *Exhibit B* attracted controversy. The concept of the installation was a series of twelve *tableaux vivants* depicting different aspects of the colonial and postcolonial oppression of black people by white people. In Bailey's words, 'Rather than portraying "the native in his natural surrounds" as human zoos did, each installation shows the brutality subjected upon asylum seekers in the EU or inflicted upon colonial subjects' (Bailey, 'Yes, Exhibit B is challenging'). In its journey across Europe, the precise composition of the *tableaux* changed to reflect that country's colonial history. Thus, in Berlin and Brussels, some parts of the installation referenced by name cases of illegal immigrants who had been forcibly deported and had died on flights home, and other scenes referred to sexual violence in events from German and Belgian colonial history (Chickha and Arnaut, p. 672). In Edinburgh, 'the brief story of a Kenyan man castrated during the Mau Mau uprisings in the 1950s is set among the bone china of a genteel English afternoon tea' (Gardner, 'Exhibit B...').

Although it has since been claimed as a *cause célèbre* for anti-censorship campaigners and libertarians (see Hume, l. 1004), with hindsight there are clear dangers with such an installation that in seeking to critique the white supremacist concept of the 'human zoo' by invoking or depicting it, an artist runs the risk of being seen to replicate or endorse that very concept. This can still happen despite the repeatedly and clearly stated intentions of the artist and despite the awareness and approval of the locally recruited performers who took part (many of their testimonials were displayed on Bailey's Facebook page). Nor can the intentions behind the work prevent some members of the audience from reacting to its structural properties, by making objectifying remarks about the semi-naked women on display, as apparently happened in Poland (Andrews, 'Exhibit B, the human zoo, is a grotesque parody'). Bailey's own role in the installation, as he reportedly 'skulks around during performances, gauging the reactions of the audience', somehow doesn't help, because it seems to confirm that responses have to be monitored and policed (Molefe, 'Racism and the Barbican's Exhibit B').

To better understand the degree of anger that this postmodern 'human zoo' concept attracted, we need to look at how these displays functioned during the age of European imperialism. Displays of indigenous people were particularly popular in the nineteenth and early twentieth centuries. They had their origins in anthropological exhibitions held at the Jardin d'Acclimatation in Paris, where in 1877 'Fourteen Nubians were presented to a fascinated Parisian public' (Greenhalgh, p. 86). However, whatever scientific motives and compunctions the Jardin had, the trend was quickly picked up and massively expanded by the international exhibitions of the late nineteenth century. The Great Exhibitions (known as *Expositions Universelles* to the French, and World's Fairs to the United States) were an international phenomenon from the mid-Victorian period up to the eve of the Second World War, in which imperial powers demonstrated their command of the world's resources (and, in the case of human exhibitions, sought to morally justify colonial exploitation by illustrating the 'degenerate' and 'backward' nature of indigenous peoples, who were presented as in need of civilizing by European empires). Beginning with the Paris Exposition of 1889, colonial peoples were established in transplanted 'native villages' within the exhibition centre itself, often living there for the six months' duration of the exposition. They were expected to build their own dwellings, make their own food and their own clothes and to 'perform religious rituals at set times each day for the visitors and to give demonstrations of their various arts and crafts' (p. 83). As Chikha and Arnaut put it, the human zoo thus 'operated in a process in which "caging" and "staging" were conjugated' (p. 667). In some ways, 'native villages' and other Great Exhibition staples such as the *Rue des Caires* (Cairo Street) – a recreation of an Egyptian street

with shops, a bazaar, camels, barbers and small theatres
for viewing 'erotic belly-dancers' – anticipate the immersive or site-specific theatre practices of the twenty-first
century (Greenhalgh, p. 103). It could be said that this is
where *Exhibit B* hit problems. It was deliberately staging an
encounter between one century's acceptable form of entertainment, the supposedly 'educational display', and that of
another century, the 'art installation'.

I've chosen to begin with the case of *Exhibit B* because
it's an extreme example of the difficulties of representing
the workings of imperialism and colonialism within a performance environment. Not all theatre about empire today
will choose such a discredited ethnographic form in which
to work. But every depiction of an imperial encounter has
to reckon with the centuries of stage depictions of 'sav-
ages', cannibals, sultans, stage Irishmen, stage Chinese and
'Indian Queens' (see Orr, pp. 109–31, 141–3).

Defining Empire

As I mentioned at the beginning, 'empire' (and the related
terms colony, colonialism, imperialist and imperialism) is a notoriously difficult concept to pin down. The
British Empire, the Roman Empire, the Inca Empire and
the Ottoman Empire may share a common conventional
descriptor, but they denote radically different principles and
ideals. John Darwin offers, as a basic definition of empire,
'The assertion of mastery (by influence or rule) by one ethnic group, or its rulers, over a number of others', and adds
that under this definition, empire has been 'the default mode

of state organisation' for most of world history (*Unfinished Empire*, l. 284). Stephen Howe, after some deliberation, offers a 'basic, consensus definition' that an empire is 'a large political body which rules over territories outside its original border'; they can be land-based, sea-based, or a combination of both, and always involve some combination of direct and indirect rule (l. 461, l. 476). Anthony Pagden helpfully sets out his four common denominators of empire: that an empire is relatively large; that it believes itself to be, at least potentially, universal; that that one ethnic or tribal group rules over several others; and that empires are usually acquired by conquest (p. 1). Unsurprisingly, Pagden rejects the notion of American imperialism, calling the United States 'very un-imperial' and intolerant of 'any kind of colonialism' (p. 35).

The word 'empire' itself is so flexible that most theorists and historians have felt the need to split it into subcategories. So, Catherine Hall distinguishes the empire of commerce and the seas from the territorial empire of conquest and settlement (p. 199), and John Darwin subdivides the British Empire into the empire of slavery, the empire of migrants, the empire of free trade, the empire of Christ and the empire of coaling stations, bases and fortresses (*Unfinished Empire*, ll. 397–409). Immerman suggests a distinction between multicultural and homogenizing empires (l. 351), while Loomba, sticking with 'colonialism' rather than empire as the overarching term, comprehensively offers administrative versus settler colonialism, plantation colonialism, annexation colonialism and neo-colonialism (pp. 23–5). Alongside such attempts at definition and redefinition, these writers also throw out asides suggesting the concept of empire makes very little sense anyway. What can we reliably say about empire if, for example, the British Empire, the largest empire that the world has ever known, in many ways does not qualify for the theoretical definition of an empire? Darwin concedes that there are good grounds for thinking the British Empire had 'no logic at all' (*The Empire Project*, l. 160), while Kwasi Kwarteng regards empire as an 'intensely pragmatic affair', with the British Empire paradoxically relying on both anarchic individualism (the 'man on the spot' making his own decisions) and extreme, hierarchical gradations (l. 153, l. 158). Piers Brendon calls the empire 'John Bull's haphazard miscellany of overseas dominions' and 'such a gallimaufry that some authorities say it never really existed at all' (p. 58, p. 98). Stephen Howe asks, 'was there, in any real sense, a singular "British empire" at any one time, let alone across time?' (l. 1264); Sarah Stockwell affirms that 'there was not one British empire but several' (p. 271).

Indeed, empire as a concept has a chimeric quality. Depending on your point of view and which logic you follow, seemingly either almost everything is an empire or nothing is. Theatre historian Marty Gould works with both a narrow and a broad definition of empire (p. 4). Darwin criticizes the assumption that empires are abnormal, monstrous or aberrant, insisting that empires have been the norm over most of world history (*Unfinished Empire*, l. 284), and that to suggest otherwise is unforgivably Eurocentric. Offering an opposing perspective, Kwarteng insists that much of the instability in the world today is specifically attributable to the British Empire's 'legacy of individualism and haphazard policy making' (l. 241). So, by some measures, empire, and the British Empire's legacy, is everywhere, even if it was hardly a 'real' empire to begin with. Another way to attempt to come to terms with this elusive concept is by considering it not as an entity but as a 'wide range of practices', an un-forming and re-forming of communities by practices including 'trade, settlement, plunder, negotiation, warfare, genocide, and enslavement' (Loomba, p. 20).

Theories of Empire

Now I want to move from definitions of empire to explanations of how modern empires work in order to set up the theatrical analysis that will follow. In the eighteenth century, it was received wisdom among political economists that the expansion of commerce would lead to fewer wars; but it was also understood, by thinkers like Immanuel Kant (1724–1804) and Adam Smith (1723–1790), that the European nations benefited most from their trading relationships with the colonies (Pagden, p. 23). In the nineteenth century, Karl Marx turned that assumption on its head, seeing colonialism as the brutal but necessary precondition for the liberation of the proletariat; it will lead to 'the commercial war of the European nations, with the globe for a theatre' (2008, p. 376). Later, Marxist thinkers like V.I. Lenin and Rosa Luxemburg built on Marx's analysis. Luxemburg, in *The Accumulation of Capital* (1913), developed the idea of capitalism seeking out new markets: 'Imperialism is the political expression of the accumulation of capital in its competitive struggle for what remains still open of the non-capitalist environment' (p. 426). Luxemburg still subscribed to the Marxist belief in the inevitable downfall of capitalism and saw imperialism as crucial to accelerating that process (pp. 426–7). And some of her remarks on economic imperialism seem to anticipate the global reach of bodies like the IMF and the World Bank today: 'Though foreign loans are indispensable for the emancipation of the rising capitalist states, they are yet the surest ties by which the old capitalist states retain their influence, exercise financial control and exert pressure on the customs, foreign and commercial policy of the young capitalist states' (p. 401).

Marxist thinkers like Aimé Césaire and Frantz Fanon in the mid-twentieth century – as France violently attempted to maintain its Algerian colony – added an understanding of how racism mapped onto the class struggle; as Fanon puts it, 'a Marxist analysis should always be slightly stretched when it comes to addressing the colonial issue', since 'it is clear that what divides this world is first and foremost what species, what race one belongs to' (p. 5). That racial hierarchies functioned as the justification for capitalism's expansion is now a widely accepted theory – one made manifest in the anthropological exhibitions discussed earlier – and, of course, it is this racial dimension of empire that has been one of its most culturally damaging legacies.

Fanon and his contemporary Kwame Nkrumah were also well aware of the development of neo-colonialism, what Nkrumah calls 'imperialism in its final and perhaps most dangerous phase' (p. ix). Indeed, many of the practices that we now consider as central to globalization were called neo-colonialism when they first appeared at the end of the period of 'official', or European, colonization. As Nkrumah explains, under neo-colonialism, 'foreign capital is used for the exploitation rather than for the development of the less developed parts of the world'; moreover, it's possible to exercise neo-colonial control as 'a consortium of financial interests which are not specifically identifiable with any particular State' (p. x). The picture that Nkrumah draws, of multinational corporations exploiting the cheap labour, resources, lax safety standards, legislative loopholes and poor worker rights of developing countries, and thereby 'export[ing] the social conflicts of the capitalist countries', will sound familiar to readers today. The irony did not escape these writers, even then, that while the United States styled itself as the friend of the formerly colonized nations, it was contributing to a form of economic imperialism that was all the more insidious because it was deemed unremarkable, just the way things were.

We might trace the development of another way of thinking about empire by starting with the ideas of the Swiss political theorist Benjamin Constant (1767–1830), who saw all empires as essentially unsustainable, and doomed to collapse into tyranny, despite the claims to legitimate rule that the imperialists might make (Pagden, p. 24). For Constant, Napoleon's failed ambition to make Europe an empire created a new Europe, after the Congress of Vienna in 1815, of self-conscious nation states that began to compete with each other for the status and economic benefits of building an empire (p. 25). Imperialism thus became a powerful political tool for manipulating public opinion at home by playing up the commercial benefits of empire and endorsing a form of competition between nations. Writing a century later, amidst the global upheavals initiated by the First World War, the Austrian economist Joseph Schumpeter argued that empires didn't serve national interests at all. In his essay 'The Sociology of Imperialism' (1919), he places himself in opposition to both Constant and Marxist thinkers like Luxemburg. Schumpeter insists that 'capitalism is by nature anti-imperialist', that imperialist tendencies are 'carried into the world of capitalism from the outside' (p. 73), and that '[t]he type of industrial worker created by capitalism is always vigorously anti-imperialist' (p. 71). In other words, imperialism can't be seen as a natural extension of capitalism; rather, it interferes with capitalist production, since wars are enormously disruptive. It's easy to see how, in the aftermath of the Great War, a particular type of nationalist imperialism, which is 'threatening Europe with the constant danger of war' might seem like the only kind of imperialism (p. 97). And there's a sense in which Schumpeter is also reacting against thinkers of the 1890s such as Paul Leroy-Beaulieu, who had (very complacently, in hindsight) argued that the competition for overseas empires in the last decades of the nineteenth century had ensured peace in Europe (Pagden, p. 26).

Schumpeter's essay starts from the assumption that imperialism is a primitive urge: 'Driven out everywhere else, the irrational seeks refuge in nationalism – the irrational which consists of belligerence, the need to hate, a goodly quota of inchoate idealism, the most naïve (and hence also the most unrestrained) egotism' (p. 12). Although he is confident that humanity will outgrow such atavistic tendencies, his ideas here are tantalisingly close to those of his fellow Austrian Sigmund Freud.

Since the turn of the millennium, Michael Hardt and Antonio Negri's book *Empire* has drawn a great deal of attention for its argument that 'Empire' today is a global network of control; conflict between imperialist powers has been replaced by 'a single power that over determines them all, structures them in a unitary way, and treats them under one common notion of right that is decidedly postcolonial and postimperialist' (p. 9). This power, however, is just as able to be repurposed, and to be used for better ends, by 'the multitude' as it is by the forces of oppression: 'The creative forces of the multitude that sustain empire are also capable of autonomously constructing a counter-Empire, an alternative political organisation of global flows and exchanges' (p. iii). It's a seductive theory, made, I think, unnecessarily complicated by Hardt and Negri's use of the words 'Empire' and 'imperial' to describe the system that they perceive, while insisting that the old empires are irrelevant. At times, too, they appear to be stepping inside the worldview of Empire in order to describe it, which adds to the confusion (p. xiv). Elements of Hardt and Negri's incitements to resistance could be seen to have filtered through to the 'Occupy' movements that sprang up in the wake of the global banking crisis and recession of 2007 onwards. Nevertheless, a particular difficulty of Hardt and Negri's empire is that often (though not always) the networked powers it describes are those primarily of the United States. By obscuring the activities of the United States within the larger framework of 'Empire', Hardt and Negri are open to accusations of underplaying American global hegemony. They claim that the 'distinct national colors of the imperialist map of the world have merged and blended in the imperial global rainbow' (p. xiii). The idea of their empire being decentred, with multiple flows, serves somewhat to disguise the habitual flow of wealth and resources from the global south to the global north, along pathways that often bear the traces of the old empires. Not all global cities, not all imperial metropolises have the same value and, indeed, the same cultural capital.

Thinking across Empire and Theatre, Theatre and Empire

Having explored at some length what we mean by empire, it's time to think about how it intersects with theatre. Although this book will focus mainly on scripted drama, staged in the UK from the decolonization period to the present, there are several other productive ways of thinking about theatres and empires, and these will also inform the analyses of plays in the second half of the book.

When we think of theatre and empire, what might immediately spring to mind is the large number of theatres dating from the nineteenth and early twentieth centuries, called 'the empire', and often first operating as music halls. The Hackney Empire (1901), the Sunderland Empire (1907) and the Liverpool Empire (1925) are among the best-known of those still standing today. In particular, as Claire Cochrane observes, those designed by Frank Matcham in the last third of the nineteenth century, 'the high noon of British imperialism', were 'flamboyant, gilded palaces of recreation', their mix of exotic influences 'taking audiences on a virtual journey through European baroque and rococo and onwards to the eastern outposts of empire ... it seems no coincidence that the chain of variety theatres he built for Edward Moss and Oswald Stoll were 'Empires'. The Edinburgh Empire was decorated with any number of golden elephants and Nubian riders' (pp. 40–1).

On the stages of these theatres, the Empire was also a near-ubiquitous presence. As Marty Gould puts it, 'it was in the theatre and related venues of popular spectacle that Britons came to see themselves as masters of an imperial domain' (p. 2). While there were many popular plays in the Victorian period that attempted to portray the complexities of particular imperial conflicts, there were also hundreds of spectacular melodramas on military or imperial themes, 'ending on a patriotic display of flags and cannon to the tune of "Rule, Britannia"' (Bratton, p. 22). There were theatres that specialized in nautical and military spectacles, like the Surrey, Astley's and Sadler's Wells, and panoramas, dioramas and cosmoramas on imperial themes; indeed, panoramas were used to popularize the idea of immigration to Australia and New Zealand in the 1840s and 1850s

(MacKenzie, p. 46). There were late-Victorian musical comedies set in India, with titles like *The Saucy Nabob, The Mahatma* and *The Begum's Diamonds* (p. 49), and the so-called Indian Mutiny (the Sepoy Rebellion of 1857) was still being dramatized for theatres forty years after the events (Gould, p. 2).

In addition to this jingoistic fare, there were Victorian theatrical melodramas that were concerned to provide a factual basis for their depictions of empire, making melodrama more like 'rational recreation' and narrowing the gap between the theatre and the halls of the Great Exhibitions (Holder, p. 133; see also Hays, pp. 139–42). Gould cites the example of Augustus Harris's play about General Gordon, *Human Nature,* at Drury Lane in 1895, which featured items on display in the foyer from the Sudan conflict, revealing Harris's 'conscious and calculated merging of entertainment with education' (p. 22).

The connections between theatre and empire also flowed in the opposite direction, as British theatre companies toured the Empire. Henry Irving, for example, brought his Lyceum Company to Canada, as well as the United States, in 1883, 1884 and 1893. A hit play like Brandon Thomas's *Charley's Aunt* (1892) could tour to South Africa, Canada and New Zealand (Brandon Thomas, p. 220). There were also British theatre repertories being performed across the empire by colonizers. The basis of Timberlake Wertenbaker's play *Our Country's Good* is an Australian performance of Farquhar's *The Recruiting Officer,* which took place as early as 1789 (a playbill survives of a performance in

Sydney in 1800 [Feldman, p. 161]). Theatres seem to have been established at an early stage of colonial settlements. Indian cities like Lucknow and Calcutta in the nineteenth century had active literary, musical and theatrical cultures (Levine l. 1706). For instance, a commercial theatre company was established in Calcutta in 1872, and western-style Bengali plays had been staged by 1795 (Chatterjee, p. 30, p. 19). Henry Morton Stanley records that on his return to Cape Colony with his escort of Wagwana ['Freedmen'] after his expedition to find the sources of the Nile, under the auspices of Lady Frere and Commodore Sullivan, 'A special evening was devoted to [the Wagwana] at the theatre, at which the acrobats received thunderous applause' (Stanley, vol. 2, p. 475). In the late nineteenth and early twentieth centuries, Canada, in turn, developed its own tradition of patriotic pageants produced annually at the Canadian National Exhibition in Toronto, including reproductions of imperial battles like 'The Siege of Pekin' (1887), 'The Siege of Sebastopol' (1888) and 'The Siege of Mafeking' (1900); indeed, the pageants began to function as 'a form of popular reportage' (Filewod p. 60).

We've already seen how the anthropological display of indigenous people took off in France. The British soon copied these ideas for their imperial exhibitions, making them even more theatrical. Under the influence of the impresario (and former music hall entertainer) Imre Kiralfy, any pretences to education and philanthropy were forgotten as the 'native village' gave way to extravaganzas like *India* at the Empress Theatre, Earls Court, a 6,000 seat theatre – the

largest theatre ever built in Britain – which formed part of
the Empire of India Exhibition in 1895 (Gregory, pp. 152–4).
This was followed by a sequence of exhibition spectaculars
culminating in *Our Indian Empire*, an 'Alfresco Spectacular'
staged at the 1908 Franco-British Exhibition, which took
place in an open-air theatre, had a cast of hundreds and ran
for two hours twice daily 'to explain', as Greenhalgh drily
notes, 'how the British civilized India' (p. 92).

Occasionally, the contact between theatre and the
empire produced some strange performative reversals. In
initial encounters with African peoples, colonialists would
play up to their assertions of kingliness: a German officer
in 1890 presented gifts from the Kaiser to Chief Ryndi of
the Chagga, including a coronation cloak from the Berlin
Opera House and 'the helmet under which Niemann once
sang Lohengrin' (Ranger, p. 229). Predictably, after this
initial period of flattery, once the colonial powers felt more
secure in Africa they withdrew their favour so that the displaced African 'paramounts' used crowns and thrones to
try to maintain their authority in the eyes of their people
(Ranger, p. 240). Hence, a relationship that began with
the presentation of theatrical props as real developed into
one where a 'puppet ruler' relies on props to enact a now-
fictional authority.

Imre Kiralfy's theatrical representations of India for
the great exhibitions, meanwhile, had already been pre-
figured by the Empire's own invented ceremonials, such
as the Durbar, which was derived from the court rituals
of the Mughal Emperors and adapted by the British in the

early nineteenth century (Cohn, p. 168). A ritual event, the Imperial Assemblage, was held in 1877 to proclaim Queen Victorian Empress of India, attended by at least 84,000 people. According to Bernard S. Cohn, the Assemblage made extensive use of theatrical effects to impress the majesty of imperial rule upon the subcontinent, despite – or perhaps because of – the absence of the monarch herself: 'The viceroy and his small party, including his wife, rode into the amphitheatre to the "March from Tannhäuser". As they got down from the carriage six trumpeters, attired in medieval costume, blew a fanfare. The viceroy then mounted to the throne to the strains of the National Anthem' (p. 204).

Empire as Rehearsal, Empire as Performance

Reading about such displays of Wagnerian pomp, it is tempting to view empire as an inherently theatrical project and to see imperial culture as suffused with practices of rehearsal and performance. George Orwell's famous essay 'Shooting an Elephant', reflecting on his time as an imperial police officer in Burma, hints at this performativity: 'at that moment, with the crowd watching me, I was not afraid in the ordinary sense, as I would have been if I had been alone. A white man mustn't be frightened in front of "natives"; and so, in general, he isn't frightened' (p. 29).

By 'rehearsal for empire', I'm thinking of the ways in which children and young people, from the later nineteenth century, were brought up not only to revere the empire, but to imagine playing their part in its perpetuation. Composers produced popular sheet music with fantasias on the Indian

Mutiny and the Ashanti War, while brass bands – with their standard repertory of military marches and patriotic songs – grew in popularity. Films were shown in music halls, theatres and churches, and public lectures on missionary work were presented with slide shows. There were toy soldiers for children to play with, of course, and by the end of the nineteenth century, the firm Britain's had a full range of British, Indian and colonial regiments as well as allies, enemies and 'ethnic' fighters (MacKenzie, p. 28). Children were also drilled at school, and the revelation of the poor health of Boer War recruits led to the development of school rifle clubs (pp. 228–9). It became an established principle of public school life that the sports field was preparation for the imperial life overseas, an idea given poetic form by Henry Newbolt's 'Vitaï Lampada': 'Play up! play up! and play the game!'. The Empire Day Movement and the Empire Youth Movement continued to be active right up to the 1950s; as well as the Cadet forces, there were the military-themed organizations like Church Lads' Brigades and the Boys' Brigade. Most successfully, there was the Boy Scouts, founded by Robert Baden-Powell, veteran of the Second Matabele War and the siege of Mafeking. The Scout movement epitomized the idea of boyhood as a rehearsal for imperial service; its motto, after all, was 'Be Prepared', and its foundational text, *Scouting for Boys*, was actually based on a military scouting manual that Baden-Powell had published in 1899.

In another sense, empire becomes a strange, dislocated performance in the early nineteenth century because communication technology had not yet caught up with the global reach of the British Empire. Thus, as Peter Putnis explains, during the Napoleonic Wars, the newspapers arriving in Australia were sometimes a year or more out of date, so that when two Spanish merchant ships captured off the coast of Peru were brought to New South Wales, no one could be sure whether Britain and Spain were at war. The Governor allowed them to be escorted into Sydney harbour as if they were friendly vessels, when in fact Britain and Spain had been at war for four months at that point (p. 157).

Empire and Culture

Having just indicated some of the ways that empire was part of the cultural landscape for British people growing up in the nineteenth and twentieth centuries, I now want to look at how cultural domination by imperial powers has been presented in recent theatre of empire. Here I'm using culture in a broad sense that includes art, law, custom and religion (Tomlinson, pp. 4–5). Theatre, perhaps because it's a cultural industry itself, has tended to focus strongly on cultural imperialism, following Edward Said's argument that the era of high imperialism has 'in one way or another continued to exert considerable cultural influence on the present' as what he calls a 'highly conflictual texture of culture, ideology and policy [which] still exercises tremendous force' (p. 5, p. 11). In the theatres of the eighteenth and nineteenth centuries, as we saw earlier, 'Empire-building was thus not just a political or military concern, but a cultural project' (Gould, p. 1). Theatrical propaganda became a means by which the economic realities of empire were represented to domestic audiences as adventure, as a civilizing mission and as the necessary defence of Britain's honour.

In reacting against these imperialist myths, playwrights since decolonization have occasionally gone to the other extreme, implying that any cultural contact between indigenous and imperial forces is catastrophic. Howard Brenton, for instance, in discussing his play *The Romans in Britain,* says that for the Celts, their violent encounter with the Romans is 'the end of their culture, its touch is death' (*The Romans in Britain*, p. vii). Despite Brenton's refusal to idealize Celtic culture in the play itself, and despite his insistence that there are 'no "goodies" and "baddies"... no obvious, or usual, "moral message"' (p. viii), the Romans are unusually clear about their intentions. Caesar announces to the Celts:

> Listen listen to me! On the mainland I burn your temples. Your priests that will not serve the Roman Gods – I kill. I desecrate their bodies. Desecration according to your beliefs. The head off and burnt, etcetera. Because there are new Gods now. Do you understand? The old Gods are dead. (p. 49)

This idea that an indigenous culture dies with 'one touch' may work as a metaphor, calling on associations with the diseases that killed large numbers of Native Americans when Spanish and English colonists arrived: smallpox, measles, influenza and the bubonic plague. It could also be associated with an event like the Tasmanian genocide, committed by the British in the first half of the nineteenth century. And it's an ideological inversion of the notion that Europeans are contaminated by any contact with indigenous people and their culture; as Hardt and Negri summarize the idea, 'Physical contamination, moral corruption, madness: the darkness of the colonial territories is contagious, and the Europeans are always at risk' (p. 199). Nevertheless, reversing that logic of contagion and saying that the Europeans are the polluters doesn't really help us to think about morality and empire in a more nuanced way. Most theatre about empires operates in the ethical shades of grey in which people negotiate their day-to-day existence under invasion, colonization and occupation. As Kelly remarks of Imperial Rome, the choice was never a straightforward one between collusion and opposition; 'it is only those who have never been subject to conquest who can afford to think in such clear-cut terms' (l. 1220). Once there was a colonial presence in a country, domination was often achieved through a combination of coercion and consent, with one or more indigenous groups typically being offered incentives by the colonists to support the deposition of the current rulers (Loomba, pp. 49–50).

In a famous essay, 'Can the Subaltern Speak?', Gayatri Chakravorty Spivak argues that there are voices of colonial subjects that have been erased from the record and which are impossible to recover (pp. 40–1). In a sense, the first part of *The Romans in Britain* attempts such an act of imaginative recovery. Brenton highlights the research that he has undertaken on the ancient Celts, even though he self-deprecatingly calls his representation of them 'highly speculative and academically suspect' (p. ix). The attempt to fill in history's blanks and give voices to the marginalized is a recurring pattern in contemporary depictions of empire. For example, Tanika Gupta's *The Empress* (RSC, The Swan, 2013) weaves together the stories of different groups of people who arrived in London on the same ship in 1887. Some of the characters, like the young Mohandas K. Gandhi and Abdul Karim (who was to become Queen Victoria's servant and confidant, the 'Munshi') will go on to become well-known historical figures, while others, like Hari, the Indian lascar, are invented characters, representing a class of forgotten workers who helped the empire to function as a global network.

Of course, there may be ethical questions raised even about this practice of imaginative recovery, since it's an attempt to 'speak for' others who cannot themselves answer back. The concept of cultural imperialism – who has the right to speak for, or on behalf of, a culture – is fraught with such complications (Tomlinson, p. 18). And, if taken to an extreme, it could be argued that any drama that represents historical events from a modern perspective is likely to represent those historical figures – be they Tamburlaine the Great, Julius Caesar, an Indian widow or a Victorian missionary – in ways that those individuals would find incomprehensible or unacceptable, were they somehow able to see themselves on stage.

It therefore follows that there is no (western) position for making theatre from which you, or I, could not possibly be accused of cultural imperialism. Even to be in the privileged position of being able to make western theatre is to participate in a dominant culture which has outlasted, displaced or exterminated other cultures. On the other hand, I'd argue that it's a valid defence of today's theatre of empire that it is concerned with redressing historical wrongs through revisionist rewritings of mainstream history. Samantha J. Carroll suggests that modern fiction that reimagines the nineteenth century from the point of view of marginalized groups, including colonial subjects, can be called 'recognitive justice'. Its purpose is not simply to induce historical or post-imperial guilt but 'to destabilise deep-structure inequalities' in contemporary culture and politics (p. 195). There is a strong strand of this seeking of recognitive justice in recent theatre of empire.

However, this is not to suggest that approaches to theatre of empire by companies, playwrights and audiences that are concerned with justice and historical wrongs should be judicial in tone. Emotional response is hugely important to the plays I'm discussing. But because of the historical framework that they employ, there sometimes seems to be a heightened critical expectation that empire plays will have a 'thesis', as though they are history essays transplanted to the stage. Helen Freshwater's analysis of the critical reaction to *The Romans in Britain* – both when it was first staged in 1980 and when it received its first major professional revival at the Sheffield Crucible in 2006 – is instructive here. A common complaint was that Brenton's play was immature, simplistic and childish (Freshwater, p. 96). Media preoccupation with the rape of one of the Celts by a Roman soldier, a *cause célè-bre* which resulted in a court case against the play's director, Michael Bogdanov, in 1981, undoubtedly affected and obscured the political content of the play (pp. 85–6, 95). By the time of the 2006 revival, the play's relevance to contemporary international events was recognized by reviewers, in line with director Sam West's insistence that the play 'can't not be about Afghanistan, Iraq, Abu Graib, Iran and the imperial attitude that says it's OK to go into another country without being asked' (qtd. in Freshwater, p. 99). Nevertheless, as Freshwater remarks, '[t]hese critical prejudices live on', and in 2006 *The Romans in Britain* was still being derided as simplistic and lacking argument (p. 98).

What concerns me about the critical reception of *The Romans in Britain* is that it seems to set the bar impossibly high for plays about empire: they must have a minutely argued interpretation of imperialism and not give way to any unnecessary or disproportionate violence or emotionalism (but of course, on the other hand, they mustn't be dull or 'worthy'). The connection that the undercover operative Thomas Chichester senses between historical empires in the second part of *The Romans in Britain* is not objective or analytical, but visionary: 'I keep on seeing the dead. A field in Ireland, a field in England … Because in my hand there's a Roman spear. A Saxon axe. A British Army machine-gun. The weapons of Rome, invaders, Empire' (p. 89). Moreover, his speech is effectively countered by O'Rourke's companion, who insists on returning the conversation from mysticism to materialism: 'Ireland's troubles are not a tragedy.

They are the crimes his country has done mine' (p. 90). Chichester's sense that our civilization is built on dead empires, and empires of the dead – and the Irishwoman's view that to simply say so, and leave it at that, blinds us to the types of imperialism that continue to this day – doesn't feel simplistic to me; it's more like a dialectic for our own day and age.

I've suggested several ways in which *The Romans in Britain* raises questions about cultural dispossession and our own position, more generally, as theatre audiences that are complicit in this. But the play is unusual in that there is little meaningful spoken interaction between the Romans and the Celts; with no common language, the Roman soldiers mock the Celts' language as 'jabber jabber' (p. 36). More frequently in plays about empire, cultural contact is represented by a developing friendship between colonizer and native that usually ends in betrayal. Such incidents illustrate the doublethink of the imperial mission to civilize: its professed aim is to transform colonized peoples, but their own lack of European culture signifies an unbridgeable gap between colonizer and native (see Loomba, p. 99). Even when they are 'like us', runs the imperial logic, they will still be other and, hence, still disposable.

This pattern of hypocrisy and betrayal is found in plays as disparate as *Raj* by Paul Swift (Leeds Playhouse Theatre in Education Company, 1982) and *The Empress* by Tanika Gupta, mentioned earlier. In both of those plays, an Indian *aya* (nanny) is dismissed and abandoned, having developed what they thought were close friendships with the British family for whom they worked. To cite some further examples, Connie, a Jamaican character in Lolita Chakrabati's *Red Velvet* (Tricycle, 2012), explains to the nineteenth-century black American actor Ira Aldridge that she was dismissed on suspicion of theft by a white mistress who had taken Connie into her confidence. And in Winsome Pinnock's *A Hero's Welcome* (Royal Court, 1989), set in the West Indies in 1947, one betrayal – Len's wife, Minda, running away to England with her lover, Stanley – leads to Len revealing an earlier betrayal. Although he had been hailed as a war hero on his return home, he had actually worked in a Liverpool munitions factory, where the English workers turned against those recruited from the empire: 'they even went on strike to get rid of us. We forgot where the real war was because we were fighting one right there' (p. 68). Thus, any idea of imperial camaraderie in working towards the Allied defeat of fascism is shown to have been sacrificed to racism and narrow self-interest. Aileen Ritchie's *The Juju Girl* (Traverse, Edinburgh, 1999) uses a dual time scheme featuring a young Glaswegian, Kate, travelling in Zimbabwe in the 1990s, who is, in turn, tracing the steps of her grandmother Catherine, the wife of a Scottish missionary in Rhodesia in the 1920s. Precious, a Shona woman who had been branded a witch by the villagers, comes to the missionaries for protection, and Catherine works to convert Precious to Christianity. But when Catherine's husband, Andrew, attempts to prove his manliness by hunting a lion that has been seen in the village, he insists on taking Precious's sweetheart, Joshua, whom Andrew carelessly loses in the mountains. Reflecting the historical complexities described at the start of this book, Ritchie also uses the 1990s plot to gently critique Scottish claims to have been 'colonised by the English too' (p. 13).

Finally, although it has been extensively analysed elsewhere – not least by Lionel Pilkington's book in this series, *Theatre & Ireland* – it is worth adding Brian Friel's classic play *Translations* to this group of theatrical representations of cultural betrayal. The English redcoats rely on Irish assistants to translate the speech of the locals of Ballybeg, even though such acts of translation, long term, will lead to the establishment of an English-only National School and the mapping of the territory with English place-names. And, on a personal level, the teacher Manus sees his pupil Maire as betraying her community, since, after her disastrous attraction to the English soldier Yolland has led to his disappearance, she wants to learn English so that she can emigrate to America. While it's possible to criticize the play as 'dissolving economic issues into the politics of language' (Loomba, p. 108), there's a calculated irony in the fact that the play is performed in English. Hence, the audience can follow everyone's conversations, misunderstandings and mistranslations, even when the characters cannot, and what's more, 'the Irish characters are obliged to speak in English to be understood by an audience, including an Irish one' a convention which makes a forceful point about the consequences of linguistic imperialism (Jones, p. 59).

Economic Imperialism

Following the idea of hegemony put forward by Antonio Gramsci (1891–1937), we would expect culture and economics to go hand in hand; the dominant economic power is able to enforce its own ideology. Economic expansion and empires, in turn, are historically related phenomena. As an example, we can look at how the (British) East India Company expanded its trading networks, and its power with local rulers, from the seventeenth century onwards. India was effectively under Company rule for a century, until Britain took direct control of the subcontinent in the wake of the 1857 rebellions. Spanish imperialism, too, 'had as much to do with economic growth as religious or military dominance'; the Spanish saw the need and the opportunity to cultivate external markets for their goods (Gasta, p. 59). The collapse of agrarian production in imperial Spain as a result of the development of international wool markets, incidentally, is the subtext to Lope de Vega's *Fuenteovejuna* (1610–14), one of the best-known and most widely performed of Spanish Golden Age dramas (see Gasta, pp. 58–99). In the nineteenth century in particular, with the growth of European nation-states, imperialism came to be considered an economic necessity that carried with it assumptions of national cultural superiority on the part of the colonizers.

Dissecting, or at least acknowledging, the economic roots of imperialism, has become more common practice in theatre of empire over the last two decades. As I've argued in a previous book, the anti-imperialist stage dramas of the 1970s tended to focus on military failures, rather than economic exploitation; these were plays like Simon Gray's *The Rear Column* (Globe Theatre, 1978) and Charles Wood's

'*H*', or *Monologues At Front of Burning Cities* (Old Vic, 1969). Such plays, in turn, reflected films of the same period that were also debunkings of British military heroism, in films as stylistically different as *The Charge of the Light Brigade* (Tony Richardson, 1968) and the second of the *Carry On* films with imperial settings, *Carry On Up the Khyber* (Gerald Thomas, 1968). Since the turn of the millennium, in the theatre, the soldier has increasingly been joined by the merchant and the trader as the carrier of imperialism.

Slavery is the most obvious and appalling instance of economic value being placed above human life. *Rough Crossings* (Birmingham Rep, 2007), Caryl Phillips' adaptation of Simon Schama's account of the foundation of Sierra Leone in the late eighteenth century, begins with one man being thrown overboard and the leader of a rebellion being shot on board a slave ship; the captain is not concerned, because 'It's all insured' (p. 28). This large-cast, epic play consistently tracks the strained relationship between principles and economics. The British, fighting the Americans in the War of Independence, encouraged the slave population of America to fight for them, with the promise of freedom at the war's end. In fact, they are abandoned in Nova Scotia, and the English abolitionist John Clarkson attempts to right this wrong by establishing a free state in Africa for the freed slaves to live in. In the play, Clarkson's idealism is contrasted sharply with the suspicions of freed slave Thomas Peters, who anticipates betrayal at every turn. And indeed, Clarkson's powers are limited, because the Sierra Leone Company, based in London, is only interested in the profitability of Freetown and treats it like just another colony. Economic interests are shown to trump individual ideals, and the standard political and economic patterns reassert themselves. By 1808, Freetown had been absorbed into the British Empire.

Staged in the year of the bicentenary of the abolition of slavery in the British Empire, *Rough Crossings* deliberately complicates and qualifies any tendency to historical complacency. Other plays from that year also reflect on the legacy of slavery. Kwame Kwei-Armah's *Statement of Regret* (National Theatre, 2007) is set in the offices of a think tank, the Institute of Black Policy Research, where its troubled founder, Kwaku Mackenzie, drives a wedge between different sections of the black community by arguing that reparations should be paid by the UK government for slavery, but should go 'to the African Caribbeans exclusively' (p. 45), since continental Africans have not suffered in the same way and were, according to his logic, complicit in the slave trade anyway. For Mackenzie, Afrocentrism that promotes the idea of Africa as a great civilization is a double insult to African-Caribbeans: 'If you were so great, why didn't you come and get us?' he argues (p. 72). Mackenzie is angry that in a perceived hierarchy of black people, African-Caribbeans are bottom of the heap, economically the worst off (his job is supported by the wealth of his Nigerian wife) and derided by Africans for supposedly having no culture of their own.

By contrast, Jimmy McGovern's *King Cotton* (Lowry, Salford, 2007) draws attention to the historical reality that during the American Civil War, the Unionist forces blockaded the ports, cutting off Manchester's supply of (slave-produced) raw cotton and causing hardship for the mill-hands. In a valiant attempt to square the circle of emphasizing working-class pride and pluck, but also placing the British industrial class struggle in the context of the absolute exploitation of slavery, the play follows two characters, mill worker Tom and runaway slave Sokoto. Tom, despite his sympathy for socialist principles, joins a man o' war financed by the mill-owners, the *Alabama*, which is sent to break the blockade and reopen the trade routes forged by slavery.

Lastly, *The Sugar Wife* by Elizabeth Kuti (Project Arts Centre, Dublin, 2005; Soho Theatre, London, 2006) also forces its audience to ask uncomfortable questions about international trade, slavery and our own complicity as consumers. The story is set in 1850. Samuel Tewkley runs a successful Dublin tea and sugar business and is branching out into coffee; his wife, Hannah, is a philanthropist and both are Quakers. Hannah has invited Alfred Darby and Sarah Worth to stay. Sarah, a freed slave from Georgia, is reputed to be an inspirational speaker on abolition; Alfred, a Yorkshireman who disowned his father's arms-manufacturing background, looks after the business side of the enterprise and pursues his interest in photography. In the conflicts and revelations that ensue, Hannah loses her illusions about her husband, their business and Alfred's altruism. She declares to Samuel: 'We have raped the world. For sugar and tea and tobacco and chocolate – for all our little pleasures – we have raped the world and everything we have flows from that, everything, every screed and stick of it' (2007, p. 76). Hannah's phrasing, that 'every screed and stick' – every speech and every piece of furniture, every possession – implicates everyone in the theatre in the colonial process that financed the expansion of the empires of Europe. And while there's a strong implication that Hannah is not at her most level-headed as she's saying these words, Samuel's blustering counterargument also fails to convince: 'We should spend out whole lives as joyless companions in guilt? Would that heal the world?' (p. 75).

King Cotton asserts, through its uncovering of a forgotten aspect of history, that although Britain may congratulate itself for abolishing slavery, what it really did in the nineteenth century was ship its conscience overseas; Britain was still willing to accept the fruits of slavery. *The Sugar Wife* takes this idea further by implying that this process continues today. Kuti makes this idea more explicit by the recurring reference to commercial brands and branding. The brand mark of the Slatebeck Iron and Steel Company, Samuel notes approvingly, decorates their pans, but he later discovers that the same dove brand adorned the guns used to herd Sarah's great-grandparents onto a slave ship (pp. 20, 51). Sarah herself, of course, as a former slave, is literally branded with a 'W': 'Stands for "Worth". Property of Worth Park, Georgia' (p. 26).

It's axiomatic that no empire can last for long if it cannot afford the costs of its own maintenance. So it's perhaps one of the absurdities of the British Empire, in hindsight, that it was so concerned to promote the cultural and moral mission of its empire – and so keen to distance this version of empire from its early days of privateers stealing Spanish gold, and the nabobs looting India – that by the early twentieth century, the British were finding it increasingly difficult to actually make money from the Empire. The Empire's expansion of territory after the First World War actually made the whole enterprise more expensive to run (Ferguson, p. 317). In two plays recounting the Suez crisis of 1956, the British Empire's dependence after the Second World War on American financial support is made plain.

Both James Graham's *Eden's Empire* (Finborough Theatre, London, 2006) and Howard Brenton's *Never So Good* (Olivier, National Theatre, 2008) come across as oddly sympathetic to the British ruling class, in part because they are now – from our present historical perspective – the hapless underdogs. In *Eden's Empire*, the US Secretary of State John Foster Dulles tells the British Prime Minister Anthony Eden that America now sees itself as 'Fighters for those who want independence from empire … We've made no secret of our dislike for colonialism and your imperial past' (l. 568). As both plays make plain, what stopped Britain and France's joint plan to take control of the Suez Canal as a 'peace-keeping force' was the United States' financial ultimatum: either Britain withdraws or the US Federal Reserve would sell sterling until Britain was forced to devalue its currency. Despite all the betrayals that the British Empire visited upon colonized peoples, what seems to grate in these two plays is that Britain fought alongside the United States in the Second World War, only for the United States to take the spoils and then disdain the British for the Empire whose soldiers had, to a considerable degree, also helped to win the war. As Ferguson concludes, '[t]he foundations of empire had been economic, and those foundations had simply been eaten up by the cost of the war' (p. 354).

Three Kinds of Empire Play

In this final part of the book, I want to take the ideas I've been exploring and develop them in relation to three kinds of contemporary theatre of empire. These are: 'the new imperium', in which historical empires are compared with present-day ones; 'empire in confined spaces', where the dramatic action is defined by colonial rules; and 'reversal and retreat', in which revolt against imperial rule forces withdrawal and, ultimately, defeat. Taken in sequence, these three groupings follow the familiar arc of the imperial drama, from discovery, to conquest and the enforcement of colonial rule, and finally, to retreat and collapse. My categories are, of course, open to debate and disagreement; other scholars and theatregoers would no doubt have their own groupings.

There's also an inevitable overlap between the three types: a play comparing empires can also be one which is set in a confined space, and shows the colonialists besieged and on the verge of collapse. To take one example, Peter Shaffer's *The Royal Hunt of the Sun* (Chichester Festival Theatre, 1964; revived at the National Theatre, 2006) concerns the Spanish conquistador Francisco Pizarro's invasion of Peru, and the Spanish slaughter of the Incas as they raided the Inca Empire for gold. There are occasional lines and situations which hint that the Spanish can be compared to later empires, especially the British in its late-Victorian missionary mode. But much of the play is also set in a confined space, as the conquistadors hold the Inca king Atahuallpa hostage while his subjects fill a huge room from floor to ceiling with gold; and the Spanish slowly realize that, if they keep their word to the king, they are essential trapped, because Atahuallpa refuses to guarantee their safe passage. This tendency for empire plays to belong, in part, to more than one of my categories is in keeping with my earlier discussion of the concept of empire, which is forever overstepping its boundaries, expanding and contracting, never quite susceptible to mapping.

The New Imperium

Empires cannot be seen in their totality. What theatre does is to pick out moments, situations, individuals, props; tiny parts that stand in for the whole. Through this synecdoche, theatre lends abstract concepts like conquest, liberty and subjugation a temporary solidity for the duration of the performance. What theatre is also able to do, by manipulation of performance space, time and action, is to pick out correspondences between empires many centuries apart. It's a form of historical vision but, as I stated earlier, it's not necessarily a fully developed historical thesis; rather, it's a felt connection, and often a means of viewing the past poetically rather than analytically.

Often in the theatre, we don't need explicit instructions to encourage us to compare one empire with another.

In David Farr's adaptation of Christopher Marlowe's *Tamburlaine the Great* (c.1587), presented as *Tamburlaine* (Bristol Old Vic, 2005), when the cast appear in black and white combat fatigues and army boots, the correspondences between the fourteenth-century Tamerlane – a Scythian shepherd who became Emperor of Persia and Central Asia – and modern empire builders, readily suggest themselves. The rest of the production avoided overlaying Tamburlaine's story with specific politic parallels. As Farr argued, the simple staging, avoiding 'the normal shields-and shouting-masquerade' served to reveal 'an existential epic' that focused on the cruelty and the humiliation of conquest, but ultimately, too, its emptiness (Farr, 'Tamburlaine wasn't censored'). As Lyn Gardner suggested, what we learn is that like any imperialist or autocrat, 'in destroying all before him – including the son he brands a coward – he unwittingly destroys himself' (Gardner, 'Tamburlaine').

The example of 'old empires for new' I've discussed at some length so far is *The Romans in Britain*. At the end of the first part of the play, a slave kills an Irish criminal in 54 BC, and is then transformed into an Irish girl throwing a stone at a patrol of British soldiers and being shot, as the Roman Army advances in British Army uniforms. It's a vivid representation of the idea that a conquered people can themselves become conquerors if a series of historical contingencies should fall into place; and of the more general idea that violence breeds violence in a seemingly endless pattern. The contrast between empires is repeated in part two of the play, but here the juxtaposition of the Thomas Chichester plot with the image of Adona, a Roman matron in 515 AD, suffering from the yellow plague, who is being carried on an improvised stretcher by two cooks, implies that the British Empire, too, in the decadent figure of Chichester, is reaching its own ignoble end. The comparison is underlined when both groups of characters talk of King Arthur, and we're shown the First Cook in the process of inventing the legend of 'a King who never was' (p. 94).

The comparison between modern empires and the ancient Roman Empire is inevitable, and recurs frequently in imperial propaganda and in the theatre. The British, from the early days of their Empire, looked back to Rome, both for self-aggrandizing comparisons and for warnings from history. As Brendon points out, Edward Gibbon's *The Decline and Fall of the Roman Empire* 'became the essential guide for Britons anxious to plot their own imperial trajectory. They found the key to understanding the British Empire in the ruins of Rome' (p. xv). After the War of Independence, George Washington and his fellow Americans embraced a Roman notion of empire; not for nothing does Washington, DC have a Capitol building and a Senate (Immerman, l. 256). Nor was Britain alone in seeking to validate its national mythology by reference to Rome; Ivan the Great called Moscow the Third Rome, and Napoleon crowned himself Emperor with a laurel wreath of gold in a ceremony based on the coronation of Charlemagne (Brendon, p. xvii). And, most notoriously, Mussolini's Italy and Nazi Germany borrowed extensively from the Roman tradition of imperial triumphs and processions, military spectacles and sporting displays.

In the theatre, Shakespeare's four plays set in Roman times – *Titus Andronicus, Julius Caesar, Antony and Cleopatra* and *Cymbeline* – have ensured that the ancient Romans have maintained a compelling onstage presence in Anglophone theatrical history. And, after the Revolution of 1688, playwrights reflected increasing English confidence as an imperial power through plays inviting comparison with Rome and about ancient Britons' resistance to Roman invasion (Orr, pp. 252–4). In seventeenth-century France, Jean Racine (1639–1699) and Pierre Corneille (1606–1684) notably dramatized episodes of Roman history – Corneille himself wrote twelve tragedies, set in periods from prehistorical Rome to the fifth century AD – which reflected France's national self-confidence, and territorial expansion, during Louis XIV's reign (Auchincloss, p. 4).

Every western nation with an empire, it seems, attempted to frame their narrative in relation to Rome. Even in decline, the principal figures of the British Empire continued to cling to Roman analogies. Harold Macmillan read Gibbon's *Decline and Fall* and famously declared the Americans the new Romans and the British the Greeks, meaning that they 'must surreptitiously direct their brash masters', though Macmillan, Chancellor of the Exchequer in the Conservative Government at the time of the Suez crisis, fatally misread President Eisenhower's intentions (Brendon, p. 492). The passing on of the Roman torch, so to speak, between Britain and the United States, is touched on in Howard Brenton's *Never So Good* and James Graham's *Eden's Empire*, both of which, as I mentioned earlier, focus extensively on the

Suez crisis and its repercussions. In *Eden's Empire*, Prime Minister Anthony Eden attempts to justify war by falsifying evidence in order to depose another country's authoritarian leader, Nasser. For the play's original 2006 audience, this will very likely have provoked memories of the 'dodgy dossier' that was used by the Labour government three years earlier to justify the invasion of Iraq and depose Saddam Hussein. In *Never So Good*, President Eisenhower mocks Harold Macmillan's talk of 'spheres of influence' and 'the imperial burden' with the words, 'Actually, America's only got one now, since the war. Just one "sphere of influence". The whole damn planet' (p. 76). Later, Eisenhower makes this mockery explicitly sexual when he refers to Britain's nuclear deterrent and accuses Macmillan of 'talking up your nuclear orgasms' (p. 88). Both plays, at fifty years' distance from the historical events they recreate, invite us to assess American post-war triumphalism in the light of all that was to follow: Vietnam, the first Gulf War, the United States' many covert interventions in Central and South American politics, and Afghanistan and Iraq.

Of course, this 'imperial changeover' is a theatrical sleight of hand; history does not shape its turning points so neatly. Historians might argue that the supposedly new American empire 'had deep roots across the world before 1945. The United States was in the global imperial mix from the moment of independence from Britain, positioning itself alongside and in contrast to the mother empire' (Burton, p. 290). Nevertheless, as I have been arguing, there is a different, more emotive force at work in contemporary theatre of empire. In the case of these plays, the interpretation of history stems from a need to make sense of – and morally evaluate – Britain's involvement in the American-led occupations of Afghanistan and Iraq. It's interesting, too – though perhaps a subject for another book – how Brenton travelled from condemnation of British imperialism in *The Romans in Britain* to an affectionate portrait of a Conservative Prime Minister who strenuously tried to defend Britain's imperial power.

In contrast to the direct representation and discussion of empires in *The Romans in Britain* and the Suez plays, Alan Wilkins' *Carthage Must Be Destroyed* (Traverse Theatre, Edinburgh, 2007) relies on the theatrical strategy of modern dress and modern speech patterns to wittily underline the connection between the American invasion of Iraq and the late Roman Republic's destruction, looting and annexation of Carthage. The analogy is deliberately not exact; there's a compelling story of individual ambition and weakness in the rise of Marcus, the fall of Gregor, and the breathtaking hypocrisy of Cato the Elder.

Nevertheless, the talk of resolutions (p. 16), of Carthage as a 'threat to the security' of the Republic (p. 17) and of a ledger, supporting this view, supposedly containing 'incontrovertible' evidence (p. 26), echoes some of the key stages in the Anglo-American route to war in Iraq.

The theatrical event of recent years that most explicitly and extensively explores the imperial legacy of Britain and the United States in the Middle East is *The Great Game: Afghanistan* (Tricycle, 2009), a cycle of plays by a dozen

British playwrights charting Afghanistan's history from the First Afghan War in 1842, via the Soviet invasion during the Cold War, to present-day US-led invasion, occupation and reconstruction. The plays were performed over a single day and complemented by verbatim pieces and monologues. In 2010, *The Great Game* was taken on a tour of the United States. A couple of examples will suffice to show how the depiction of military intervention in Afghanistan resonated with both contemporary and historical concerns. In the first play, Stephen Jeffreys' 'Bugles at the Gates of Jalalabad', the realist English soldier Hendrick remarks of the First Afghan War that 'It is our job to fight cheap wars so that our people back home can live expensive lives. There was a mistake. It has been an expensive war' (p. 27). While Hendrick refers to the lives of the Victorian upper classes, the line emphasizes the neo-colonial idea of social problems being exported abroad, and ruthlessly strips the ideology of (neo-)imperialism down to a question of global economics. In David Greig's 'Miniskirts of Kabul', by contrast, we are shown an imagined conversation between a Writer and the former President of Afghanistan, Najibullah, in the UN Compound in Kabul in 1996, shortly before his death at the hands of the Taliban. So, Najibullah's remark that 'Every bloody conflict in the world today has its origins in the imagination of British surveyors' might seem to connect with the themes of Ron Hutchinson's 'Durand's Line' (the second play in the cycle). But in fact, everything that is said in Greig's play is imagined, provisional, including both the Writer's rejection of the British Empire and Najibullah's refusal to believe that

theatre&empire

in her 'heart of hearts' she doesn't still hold on to imperial values (pp. 134–5). The accusation is permanently poised between an external accusation and a western liberal's self-accusation. Like Naomi Wallace's contribution to the series, 'No Such Cold Thing' – also a break with realism – Greig reasserts the imaginative, conjectural, constructed quality of the history that *The Great Game* shows us. However much we know factually about Afghanistan's history, we can't have access to the consciousness of the victims of clashing empires and regimes in their last moments alive.

The comparison between old empires and new implies a view of history along the lines of Schumpeter's sense that imperialism represents an atavistic urge in modern humanity. Yet these plays don't share Schumpeter's confidence that humanity will outgrow and evolve away from imperialism. At times, the sense of history repeating itself can shade into absurdity. In D.C. Moore's *The Empire* (Royal Court, 2010), set in Helmand Province, Afghanistan, in 2006, three British soldiers try to piece together what a British Pakistani, Zia, was doing apparently fighting for the Taliban. Zia's explanations seem unreliable and contradictory, and we, and the soldiers, have no means of verifying them. Finally, Gary, a Lance Corporal whose friend dies of his injuries from the Taliban attack, delivers an outburst to his Captain, Simon, encapsulating his understanding of how British imperialism has intersected with race and class for generations:

> Yeah, way it is, Like. My dad. He's an old fucker.
> He was in Aden. Doing shit like this. For cunts

like you. And my grandad. India. And it's. Thick
cunts, led by posh cunts, hitting brown cunts.
Way it is. Even now. (p. 88)

As the play ends with the arrival of a Chinook helicopter,
everyone may be implicated in Zia's brutal beating, and everyone has been pushed beyond their limits of endurance.
'What the fuck do we do?' asks Gary, and his commanding
officer doesn't have an answer.

Empires in Confined Spaces

The second type of theatre of empire I want to highlight consists of plays and productions where colonial rules dictate
that everyone has to stay in one place. It's easy to see why
plays dealing with confinement should be popular in modern
theatre of empire for practical reasons. Showing empire in a
confined space solves the staging problems, and the expense,
of depicting pitched battles, artillery fire, and the sacking
and looting of cities. A simplified setting and a smaller cast
allow empire to be viewed in microcosm, to swap the epic for
the realist mode. Like the comparison between old and new
empires, limiting the action to a strictly defined space allows
the workings of empire to be made visible and concrete.
And, like the expanding and contracting definition of empire
given earlier, these plays take an expansive world-system and
concentrate its workings into the interactions of individuals
in a room, house, settlement, town, colony or ship.

Let's look at some examples. *Our Country's Good*
(Royal Court, 1984), written by Timberlake Wertenbaker

and directed by Max Stafford-Clark, is perhaps the classic play about empire and confinement, its influence magnified not only by commercial success but by its inclusion on British GCSE exam syllabi. It's set in Botany Bay as the first convict fleet arrives in Australia with its military guard; Major Ross regards it as 'a hateful, hary-scary, topsy-turvy outpost, this is not a civilisation'; and, as the convict Arscott forcefully insists, holding his useless paper compass, 'There's no escape' (p. 34). Though initially the play was praised by reviewers, as the play transferred to Australia and London's West End, it was criticized for its apparently exclusive concern with English identity, for its failure 'to present the actual victims of colonisation in Australia in any more than gestural terms' (Feldman, pp. 153–4). Nadia Fall's revival of *Our Country's Good* on the National Theatre's Olivier stage in 2015 tried to redress this balance, showing the unnamed Aborigine of Wertenbaker's script performing rituals and weaving unnoticed through stage space during the colonists' scenes. As an audience, we're never allowed to regard Sydney Cove as uninhabited at the colony's point of arrival.

Our Country's Good belongs to a network of plays which develop the 'white settler' motif. Nine years earlier, there was Steve Gooch's *Female Transport* (Half Moon Theatre, London, 1973), set on board the convict ship, the *Sydney Cove*, bound for Australia. Twenty-five years after *Our Country's Good*, Stafford-Clark directed a sequel, of sorts, in the form of *The Convicts' Opera* by Stephen Jeffreys (Sydney Theatre, 2008; Salisbury Playhouse, 2009), in which the prisoners on a (fictional) transportation ship rehearse

John Gay's *The Beggar's Opera* (1728). And Richard Bean's *Pitcairn* (Chichester Festival Theatre, 2014) also directed by Stafford-Clark, deals with the aftermath of the mutiny on the *Bounty*, where the mutineers attempt to establish a new society on the uninhabited island of Pitcairn in the South Pacific, taking a small group of Tahitian men and women with them. Works like *Pitcairn* and *Our Country's Good* have a kind of ready-made appeal, where the attempt to establish a (brutal) form of civilization holds a certain fascination, like watching a cross between Daniel Defoe's *Robinson Crusoe* and George Orwell's *Nineteen Eighty-Four*. There are inevitable arguments over sex, rationing, discipline and hierarchy, and the inbuilt tension of how long supplies will last and whether Britain has forgotten the colonists. The dramatic formula has even been successfully adapted into a television series set in Botany Bay and written by Jimmy McGovern, *Banished* (Channel 4, 2015).

Theatre of empire in confined spaces can also turn the tables on its audience. In *The Female Transport*'s original staging, the above-deck scenes were played on a platform above the audience's heads, lending the production an immersive quality (p. 6). In Mapping4D's devised work *The Pink Bits* (Riverside Studios, Hammersmith, 2004), the audience was placed in a school room and was invited to retrieve items from their desks, and monitors patrolled the aisles while a teacher related and then began to relive the horrifying Amritsar massacre of Indian civilians by the British in 1919.

The common ancestor to these two table-turning productions is, I'd suggest, John Arden's *Serjeant Musgrave's Dance*

(Royal Court, 1959). The play is set in a confined space: a Victorian mining town in the north of England, cut off by road, rail and telegram by snow. The soldiers arrive, and at first the audience, as well as the townspeople, believe that they are there to drum up recruits. In fact, it emerges that Musgrave and his men are deserters from the British Army, who stole some money and a Gatling gun and went on the run back to England after a colonial massacre. The climax of the play's action takes place once the soldiers' real intent has been revealed: to preach the evils of militarism, and apparently, to slaughter the townspeople to avenge the colonial deaths they witnessed. The townspeople are held hostage in the market square, and the audience is addressed directly as if they are part of the mining community, the Gatling gun trained on them. The empire's slaughter has come home, a point graphically illustrated in the scene by the skeleton of a local boy – the sweetheart of the barmaid, Annie – which dangles behind the soldiers on the market cross.

In terms of the elements of imperialism we looked at earlier, 'empire in confined spaces' connects strongly, at various points, with both the economic and cultural aspects of empire. The scarcity of resources makes each one of these colonies, islands or ships a Little Britain, whose food, drink and privileges are inevitably distributed unevenly, according to the hierarchical priorities of the 'home' country. In *The Female Transport*, conversations between the Surgeon, the Captain and the Sergeant reveal the financial calculation at the heart of the transportation industry and – as with the slave trade – the temptation to trade human life and well-being for an increased profit margin. In *Serjeant Musgrave's Dance*, the soldiers are initially welcomed by the town's mayor as it is hoped that the army will be able to press-gang the union activists and stop the strike from interfering with industrial profits at home. Meanwhile, in *Our Country's Good*, with the recurring presence of the Aborigine, and in *Pitcairn*, with the displaced Tahitians, the appropriating culture of empire comes into inevitable conflict with indigenous cultures. And, of course, in both *Our Country's Good* and *The Convicts' Opera*, Ralph Clark and William Vaughan convert a group of colonists to the civilizing benefits of Britain's theatrical culture.

Reversal and Retreat

Finally, I want to focus on theatre that shows what happens when there's a rebellion or uprising, and the colonizers are forced to retreat: the endgame of imperialism. Typically, these are dramas about the turning point where an occupation becomes a siege.

Looking back on the incidents that the British chose to celebrate, commemorate and dramatize during the period of high imperialism, the Empire comes across as a series of debacles, lucky scrapes and last-minute rescues: an empire constantly besieged. The Morant Bay Rebellion, The Siege of Cawnpore, the Siege of Lucknow, General Gordon's Last Stand, the Battle of Rorke's Drift, the Relief of Mafeking: such stories, quickly transformed into myth in print and on stage, were immensely useful to the propaganda of empire in the nineteenth century. They made the British forces seem like plucky underdogs against the savage hordes, when the usual state of affairs was that imperial troops overwhelmed and massacred indigenous people with their firepower. As Gott has argued, 'To retain control the British were obliged to establish systems of oppression on a global scale, both brutal and sophisticated. These in turn were to create new outbreaks of revolt' (p. 2). The fact that revolts took place was then used as justification for continued imperial rule, since – the argument went – the indigenous population was clearly not ready to govern its own affairs.

By any count, the British soldiers and bureaucrats were vastly outnumbered by their colonized peoples, who numbered 200 million by 1820 (Brendon, p. 30). An often-cited statistic is that 900 British civil servants and 70,000 British soldiers somehow managed to govern more than 250 million Indians (Ferguson, p. 163). In contrast to the Roman Empire, the British didn't have a huge standing army to enforce imperial conquest (Kelly, l. 369) and so relied on (over-)reacting to rebellions once they had happened by sending in expeditionary forces and Maxim guns. This induced an undertone of anxiety among the colonialists that contrasted with the official narrative that the European empires were holding imperial possessions in trust, as custodians, until the colonized people were sufficiently developed to rule themselves. Kathryn Tidrick identifies 'the sense of nemesis with which British imperialists were periodically afflicted when they thought of their ill works in the world' (p. 268). As Frantz Fanon suggested, the colonizers were right to be anxious: 'The colonized subject is

constantly on his guard ... He is dominated but not domes-
ticated ... He patiently waits for the colonist to let his guard
down and then jumps on him. The muscles of the colonized
are always tensed' (p. 16).

The classic example of the 'jump' of the colonized subject in modern theatre of empire is in Joint Stock's *Cloud
Nine* (Royal Court, 1979), the first act of which is set in a
farcical, caricatured version of 'a British colony in Africa in
Victorian times' (p. 248). At the end of the act, the servant Joshua, who had initially proclaimed his wish to be
what white men want him to be (p. 252), 'raises his gun to
shoot CLIVE', the colonial administrator (p. 288). In the
course of the act, we follow the collapse of colonial order,
from Clive considering himself 'a father to the natives here'
(p. 251), to a sense of the rebellion and its military suppres-
sion getting ever closer and the realization, by Mrs Saunders
at least, that 'there's no place for me here' and she must
return to England (p. 287).

Cloud Nine, then, can be interpreted as a play where the
open vistas of Africa, suggesting limitless imperial ambition, are shown to narrow and tighten to the circumference
of a single house and its verandah. Its absurd aspects have
an antecedent in Boris Vian's *The Empire Builders* (Théâtre
Recamier, Paris, 1959; New Arts Theatre Club, London,
1962). In Vian's play, a mother, father, their daughter,
Zenobia, and their servant regularly have to leave their apart-
ment in the middle of the night and move to smaller, dirtier
accommodation on the next floor up of the building, as they
are pursued by a mysterious Noise. In each room, there's a

schmürz: a limping, bleeding creature, dressed in rags, whom Zenobia's parents and Mug never miss an opportunity to kick, beat, spit on or whip. The critic Martin Esslin strangely insisted that *The Empire Builders* is not an allegory for empire but rather 'a poetic image of mortality and the fear of death' (Esslin, p. 276). The evidence from the play text, though, certainly seems to support a reading that Vian is metaphorically depicting France's empire, in the context of the bloody and protracted Algerian War of Independence (1954–62). The older characters – representing old European imperialism – are plagued by amnesia, unable to make sense of their predicament, and until the final scene, the father, Leon, assiduously ignores the presence of the suffering *schmürz*; even as he hits it and shoots at it, he continues to talk to himself about flowers (p. 55). The references to the Algerian War are inescapable in two other absurdist plays of the period, Jean Genet's *The Blacks* (Théâtre de Lutece, Paris, 1959) and *The Screens* (Odéon, Paris, 1966). The reversals of racial identity and the characters shown transcending death in *The Blacks*, and the conversing with inanimate objects and caricatured depiction of the colonial officer in *The Screens* – to take a handful of examples – suggest that Genet's style may have been an influence on the opening act of *Cloud Nine*. Indeed, Churchill cites Genet in her 1983 preface to the play (*Plays 1*, p. 245).

So, modern plays of siege, retreat and the collapse of colonial order have often been characterized by absurd, repetitive or irrational action and behaviour. This is not to align all plays in this category with the 'theatre of the absurd', as first identified by Esslin. Rather, I'm suggesting that imperialism is rendered absurd when it becomes aware of the fragility of its grip on power and has nothing but the symbols of authority left (the Union Jack in *Cloud Nine*; Leon's military uniform and whip in *The Empire Builders*). As my quotation from Fanon in this section indicates, the theatre of imperial reversal and retreat is informed by anti-colonial theorists like Fanon, as well as playwrights like Genet and Césaire. In particular, the idea that the horrors of colonial rule cannot be expressed straightforwardly – that it creates irrationality both in the minds of the colonized and the colonizers – is communicated in these plays by breaks with realist convention and naturalistic performance styles. Fanon highlights at some length, in *The Wretched of the Earth*, the mental strain placed on both the colonized and the colonizer when protest and rebellion leads to clampdowns, arrests and torture. Both those agitating for independence, and the European police and soldiers pitted against them, are subject to nightmares, delusions, and visual and aural hallucinations (pp. 190–9). Colonial wars are, he writes, 'a breeding ground for mental disorders' (pp. 182 3).

British Theatre, Post-Imperialism

What, then, connects the nineteenth-century theatre of empire in all its pomp, and the theatre of empire of the twenty-first century that I've just been discussing? What's certainly true is that the tone of the theatre of empire has effectively been reversed since the jingoism of Victorian times and is now characterized by ambivalence and ambiguity, as well as anger over historical instances of white supremacist attitudes, greed and plunder, and authoritarian rule. I've noted already the tendency of modern theatre of empire to avoid definitive statements, the polemical certainties of the 'thesis play'. Perhaps the key term here is 'multiple subjectivities', as realized in the many strands of *The Empress*, *The Great Game* and even in the unresolved ambiguities of *The Empire*.

Earlier, I identified a pattern in which children and young people in the age of imperialism were consistently rehearsing for a role in the empire that was itself, partly, a performance. This pattern finds its modern parallel in plays where characters rehearse and perform plays. Alexander Feldman sees this type of play as part of a wider pattern that he calls historiographic metatheatre, which 'interrogates the possibility of exchanging official histories for alternative constructions, while simultaneously acknowledging the contingency of all historical representations' (p. 28).

In terms of production design, there is, likewise, a world of difference between the spectacular Victorian military melodramas and minutely reproduced 'native villages' of the great exhibitions and the open, flexible staging of theatre of empire today in productions like *The Great Game*, *Tamburlaine*, and *The Empress,* and *Dara* by Shahid Nadeem (Lyttelton, National Theatre, 2015), which depicts events leading up to the collapse of the Mughal Empire in seventeenth-century India. In such epic imperial narratives, flexibility and dynamism in staging are of key importance, where Victorian imperial theatre often sought to present a concrete, sometimes pseudo-scientific, sense of place.

In thinking about these contrasts and their implications for contemporary theatre, I'd highlight the work of debbie tucker green as particularly pertinent. Like Churchill before her, tucker green explores the theatrical possibilities of cross-racial and cross-gender casting. For example, in *Trade* (The Swan, Stratford-upon-Avon, 2005), a play that deals with female sex tourism in the Caribbean, three black actresses play a variety of male and female roles, including two of the central characters, the white women 'The Regular' and 'The Novice'. Such a subject, which is also central to Tanika Gupta's *Sugar Mummies* (Royal Court, 2006), suggests uncomfortable connections between the slave trade of the eighteenth century and the post-imperial trade in Caribbean men between liberated and wealthy white British women.

tucker green's *Stoning Mary* (Royal Court, 2005), meanwhile, takes situations and figures that are recognizably from post-decolonization African countries – 'The AIDS Genocide', 'The Child Soldier' – and defamiliarizes them by insisting, 'The play is set in the country it is performed in' and 'All characters are white' (p. 2). As Lynette Goddard argues, such a presentational technique 'bring[s] the issues closer to home and urge[s] the audience to consider whether these issues would be as easily ignored if they were happening in England' (p. 183). At the same time, the play enacts the imperialist's nightmare of contamination; it's a vision of colonial violence and disorder spreading back to the metropolitan centre. In *Truth and Reconciliation* (Royal Court, 2011), the sites of former conflict in which these doomed attempts at reconciliation between victims and perpetrators take place – South Africa, Zimbabwe, Rwanda, Northern Ireland – point to the continuing, baleful legacy of European colonialism on these modern nations. tucker green's plays are not empire plays in the way that most of the works discussed in this book are; they eschew historical settings and stories that posit a direct correspondence between past and present. Nevertheless, the plays I've discussed here, in their powerful and pessimistic invocation of the effects of empire, are distinctive examples of post-imperial British theatre.

Challenging the idea of a rising American empire, Lucy Kirkwood's highly successful *Chimerica* (Almeida Theatre, 2013) gives dramatic force to the idea that US global hegemony is on the wane in the face of the economic might of China. As Tess Kendrick, an English marketing profiler, explains in her moment of epiphany, midway through a PowerPoint presentation to western corporate clients: 'Because you're about to get into bed with someone you don't really understand, which is, it just seems a bit ... lunatic, because, you know, this is the future. It's the next hundred years. And we don't understand. And I think that might be a problem. Right?' (p. 110). The moment of American imperialism that has engendered such a wide-ranging theatrical reassessment of empire, and the British Empire, especially, can be read in this light as a short-term distraction from larger historical forces. As Tidrick pithily remarks, the US victory in the first Gulf War and the collapse of the Soviet Union led to 'the brief emergence in America of an explicit consciousness of itself as an imperial power' and an attempt to 'consolidate America's global power before China could challenge it' (p. xi). The folly of the Iraq War has brought an end, argues Tidrick, to America's 'flirtation with empire' (p. xii). If the economic global dominance of China is the future, then once again Hardt and Negri's empire – a 'single power that overdetermines them all' – will turn out to be yet another nation state and not so 'postimperialist' after all.

The Theatre that Empire Built

The final question I want to explore in this final section of the book is: has being a former imperial nation shaped, more generally, the kind of theatre we make today? This is a hard question to answer, because English identity has been tied to British identity for the last three centuries, and British identity has, in turn, been wrapped up in imperial identity for at least as long. Now that the British Empire has devolved into the Commonwealth, what once seemed unthinkable – the breakup of the UK – now seems, to some degree, a likely prospect. The journalist and critic Ian Jack has discussed this point of view ('Did the end of the British Empire make the death of the Union inevitable?'). The process of devolution in the UK, begun in 1998 under Tony Blair, has produced some anomalies in terms of theatre institutions. There's a National Theatre of Scotland and two Welsh National Theatre organizations – National Theatre Wales and the Welsh-language Theatr Genedlaethol

Cymru — but London's Royal National Theatre is not specifically for England.

And in so far as the theatre of empire intersects with the 'state of the nation' play — as it clearly does in plays like John Osborne's *The Entertainer* and Peter Flannery's *Our Friends in the North* — then, to that extent, the state of the nation play is also the post-imperial crisis play (Billington, pp. 102–3). (Flannery's play, curiously absent from Michael Billington's book *State of the Nation*, charts post-war political betrayals in the north-east of England and has a sub-plot which takes place during the Rhodesian Bush War [1964–79].) That said, it's easy to overgeneralize about state of the nation plays, just as it's easy to mis-identify a thesis play where no overarching thesis is intended by the playwright or company. Also, to assume an automatic association between the state of the nation play and the empire play would be rather parochial and solipsistic — as if all that talk about crimes overseas was 'really' about the British and their identity crisis.

On the other hand, the British urge to find comedy in tragedy, to deflate pompous sentiments through irony, finds its place in the self-mockery of British good intentions in plays like *Cloud Nine*, *The Juju Girl*, *Rough Crossings* and *Our Country's Good*. In fact, watching the rehearsal scenes in the 2015 revival of *Our Country's Good*, I was struck by how closely they resembled the style of a British comedy or light farce, down to immediately recognizable British character types. If it hadn't been for the period costumes, we might have been watching an Alan Ayckbourn play. So perhaps another way of thinking about the 'empire in confined spaces' strand discussed earlier is that it's a way to turn an empire play into a form of domestic comedy.

It's tempting to say that the British Empire was Britain's last big idea about its purpose and place in the world, and that since then, in international politics and in theatre, 'we' have stayed small and insular. Such a theory would point to a long-standing tradition of English pragmatism and empiricism (that is, a belief that knowledge is rooted in direct experience) as opposed to the abstract, the theoretical and the metaphysical (Ackroyd, pp. 384, 386). Hence, it could be argued, the long-standing British preference is for realist playwriting and realist staging. But any notion that theatre in the UK rejects abstraction and experimentation would have to exclude the productions of Katie Mitchell, Simon McBurney and Cheek By Jowl, as well as British receptivity, at the Barbican or the Edinburgh International Festival, to directors from continental Europe like Thomas Ostermeier or Calixto Bieito. What's more, as I hope I've demonstrated conclusively in this book, we still create ambitious, epic, large-cast sweeping narratives of empire in the UK; it's just that these are reimagined, untold stories from the other side of the imperial divide.

The US Secretary of State Dean Acheson famously observed in 1962 that 'Great Britain has lost an empire and has not yet found a role' (quoted in Ferguson, p. 365). It's a statement that has its theatrical connotations; Britain is an actor who can't find a suitable role on the world stage. But for British theatre, as I've shown, global events since 2001 have jump-started an interest in empire among a new generation of writers where once the theatre had been tongue-tied and diffident on the subject.

For Ferguson, the lesson to be drawn from Acheson's comment is that 'the Americans have taken our old role without yet facing the fact that an empire comes with it'. He borrows his phrasing from Oscar Wilde when he calls the United States 'an empire, in short, that dare not speak its name' (p. 381). 'Empire' may be, for historians and theorists, an inappropriate word to use to describe and analyse American global hegemony. If so, it's perhaps time to redefine the word in accordance with popular usage and this widely felt connection, which has nowhere been more powerfully presented than in contemporary theatre.

further reading

A great many analyses of empire, and the British Empire in particular, have been published in recent years. Philippa Levine's *The British Empire: Sunrise to Sunset* offers a wide-ranging introduction to the subject; Niall Ferguson's *Empire: How Britain Made the Modern World* is the most controversial of the recent crop. Ferguson's argument has been widely caricatured, but it's still a significant work, worth engaging with first-hand, as is its sequel, *Colossus: The Rise and Fall of the American Empire*. Richard H. Immerman's *Empire For Liberty* also adds many insightful historical perspectives to the 'is America an empire?' debate. Piers Brendon's *The Decline and Fall of the British Empire 1781–1997* is a comprehensive and highly readable account. An accessible guide to theatre and performance in the Roman Empire is Richard Beecham's *Spectacle Entertainments of Early Imperial Rome*.

In literary, political and cultural theory, Ania Loomba's *Colonialism/Postcolonialism*, now in its third edition, remains an excellent introduction to different theories of empire and how they can be applied to texts. Hardt and Negri's *Empire*, like Ferguson, is worth engaging with directly, since different readers can take very different meanings from it. Kathryn Tidrick's *Empire and the English Character* is insightful on how the English thought about empire.

There isn't much writing that deals with theatre and empire in different periods. There's a lot of published work on empire in the early modern theatre; Tristan Marshall's *Theatre and Empire: Great Britain on the London Stages under James VI and I* and Bridget Orr's *Empire on the English Stage 1660–1714* cover the period well. Marty Gould's *Nineteenth Century Theatre and the Imperial Encounter* is an absorbing exploration of Victorian theatre of empire. *Imperialism and Theatre*, edited by J. Ellen Gainor, is an important collection of essays and serves as a good introduction to the places where theatre of empire and postcolonial theatre meet and overlap.

Ackroyd, Peter (2002) *Albion: The Origins of the English Imagination*. London: Chatto & Windus.

Andrews, Kehinde (2014) 'Exhibit B, the human zoo, is a grotesque parody.' *The Guardian,* 12 September 2014, date accessed 7 August 2015 <www.theguardian.com/commentisfree/2014/sep/12/exhibit-b-human-zoo-boycott-exhibition-racial-abuse>.

Auchincloss, Louis (1996) *La Gloire : The Roman Empire of Corneille and Racine*. Columbia, S.C.: University of South Carolina Press.

Bailey, Brett (2014) 'Yes, Exhibit B is challenging – but I never sought to alienated or offend.' *The Guardian,* 24 September 2014, date accessed 7 August 2015 <www.theguardian.com/commentisfree/2014/sep/24/exhibit-b-challenging-work-never-sought-alienate-offend-brett-bailey>.

Balme, Christopher B. (1999) *Decolonizing the Stage: Theatrical Syncretism and Post-Colonial Drama*. Oxford: Clarendon Press.

Bean, Richard, Lee Blessing, David Edgar, David Greig, Amit Gupta, Ron Hutchinson, Stephen Jeffreys, Abi Morgan, Ben Ockrent, Simon Stephens, Colin Teevan, Naomi Wallace and Joy Wilkinson (2010) *The Great Game: Afghanistan*. London: Oberon.

Billington, Michael (2007) *State of the Nation: British Theatre since 1945*. London: Faber.

Brandon Thomas, Jevan (1955) *Charley's Aunt's Father: A Life of Brandon Thomas*. London: Douglas Saunders.

Bratton, J.S., Richard Allen Cave, Brendan Gregory, Hedi J. Holder, and Michael Pickering (1991) *Acts of Supremacy: The British Empire and the Stage, 1790–1930*. Manchester: Manchester University Press.

Brendon, Piers (2007) *The Decline and Fall of the British Empire: 1781–1997*. London: Jonathan Cape.

Brenton, Howard (1989) *The Romans in Britain. Plays: Two*. London: Methuen Drama, 1–95.

——— (2008) *Never So Good*. London: Nick Hern.

Burton, Antoinette (2011) *Empire in Question: Reading, Writing, and Teaching British Imperialism*. Durham: Duke University Press.

Carroll, Samantha J. (2010) 'Putting the "Neo" Back into Neo-Victorian: The Neo-Victorian Novel as Postmodern Revisionist Fiction.' *Neo-Victorian Studies* 3:2, 172–205.

Chatterjee, Sudipto (1995) 'Mise-en-(Colonial-) Scène: The Theatre of the Begal Renaissance.' *Imperialism and Theatre*. Ed. J. Ellen Gainor, 19–37.

Chikha, Chokri Ben and Karel Arnaut (2013) 'Staging/caging 'Otherness' in the Postcolony: Spectres of the Human Zoo.' *Critical Arts: South-North Cultural and Media Studies* 27:6, 661–83.

Chomsky, Noam (2012) *Making the Future: The Unipolar Imperial Moment*. London: Penguin.

Churchill, Caryl (1985) *Could Nine. Plays 1*. London: Methuen, 243–320.

Cochrane, Claire (2011) *Twentieth-Century British Theatre: Industry, Art and Empire*. Cambridge: Cambridge University Press.

Cohn, Bernard S. (1983) 'Representing Authority in Victorian India.' *The Invention of Tradition*. Eds. Hobsbawm and Ranger, 165–209.

Cox, Emma (2014) *Theatre & Migration*. Basingstoke, UK: Palgrave Macmillan.

Darwin, John (2009) *The Empire Project: The Rise and Fall of the British World-System, 1830–1970.* Cambridge: Cambridge University Press. Ebook.

———— (2012) *Unfinished Empire: The Global Expansion of Britain.* London: Penguin. Ebook.

Esslin, Martin (1980) *The Theatre of the Absurd.* Harmondsworth, UK: Penguin.

Farr, David (2005) 'Tamburlaine wasn't censored.' *The Guardian,* 25 November 2005, date accessed 18 August 2015 <http://www. theguardian.com/stage/2005/nov/25/theatre1>.

Fanon, Frantz (2004) *The Wretched of the Earth.* New York: Grove Press.

Ferguson, Niall (2004) *Empire: How Britain Made the Modern World.* London: Penguin.

Filewod, Alan (1995) 'Erect Sons and Dutiful Daughters: Imperialism, Empires and Canadian Theatre.' *Imperialism and Theatre.* Ed. J. Ellen Gainor, 56–70.

Gainor, J. Ellen, ed. (1995) *Imperialism and Theatre: Essays on World Theatre, Drama and Performance.* Abingdon, UK: Routledge.

Gardner, Lyn (2014) 'Exhibit B – facing the appalling reality of Europe's colonial past.' *The Guardian,* 12 August 2014, date accessed 7 August 2015 <www.theguardian.com/stage/2014/aug/12/ exhibit-b-edinburgh-festival-2014-review>.

————(2005) 'Tamburlaine.' *The Guardian,* 15 October 2005, date accessed 18 August 2015 <theguardian.com/culture/2005/oct/15/ theatre.art>.

Gasta, Chad M. (2013) *Imperial Stagings: Empire and Ideology in Transatlantic Theater of Early Modern Spain and the New World.* Chapel Hill, NC: University of North Carolina Press.

Goddard, Lynette (2007) *Staging Black Feminisms: Identity, Politics, Performance.* Basingstoke: Palgrave Macmillan.

Gott, Richard (2012) *Britain's Empire: Resistance, Repression and Revolt.* London: Verso.

Gould, Marty (2011) *Nineteenth Century Theatre and the Imperial Encounter.* Abingdon, UK: Routledge.

Graham, James (2006) *Eden's Empire.* London: Methuen.

Greenhalgh, Paul (1988) *Ephemeral Vistas: A History of the Expositions Universelles, Great Exhibitions and World's Fairs, 1851–1939.* Manchester: Manchester University Press.

Gregory, Brendan (1991) 'Staging British India.' *Acts of Supremacy.* 150–178.

Greig, David (2010) 'The Miniskirts of Kabul.' *The Great Game: Afghanistan,* 127–49.

Hall, Catherine (2008) 'Culture and Identity in Imperial Britain.' *The British Empire: Themes and Perspectives.* Ed. Sarah Stockwell. Oxford: Blackwell, 199–217.

Hardt, Michael and Antonio Negri (2000) *Empire.* Cambridge, MA, and London: Harvard University Press.

Hare, David (2006) *Stuff Happens.* Rev. ed. London: Faber.
———— (2008) *The Vertical Hour.* London: Faber.

Hays, Michael (1995) 'Representing Empire: Class, Culture, and the Popular Theatre in the Nineteenth Century.' *Imperialism and Theatre.* Ed. J. Ellen Gainor, 132–147.

Hobsbawm, Eric and Terence Ranger, eds (1983) *The Invention of Tradition.* Cambridge: Cambridge University Press.

Holder, Heidi J. (1991) 'Melodrama, Realism and Empire on the British Stage.' *Acts of Supremacy,* 129–49.

Howe, Stephen (2002) *Empire: A Very Short Introduction.* Oxford: Oxford University Press. Ebook.

Hulme, Mick (2005) *Trigger Warning: Is the Fear of Being Offensive Killing Free Speech?* London: William Collins. Ebook.

Immerman, Richard H. (2010) *Empire for Liberty: A History of American Imperialism from Benjamin Franklin to Paul Wolfowitz.* Princeton: Princeton University Press. Ebook.

Jeffreys, Stephen (2010) 'Bugles at the Gates of Jalalabad.' *The Great Game: Afghanistan,* 15–29.

Jones, Nesta (2000) *Brian Friel: Philadelphia, Here I Come! Translations, Making History, Dancing at Lughnasa.* London: Faber.

Kelly, Christopher (2006) *The Roman Empire: A Very Short Introduction.* Oxford: Oxford University Press. Ebook.

Kirkwood, Lucy (2013) *Chimerica.* London: Nick Hern.

Kwarteng, Kwasi (2011). *Ghosts of Empire: Britain's Legacies in the Modern World.* London: Bloomsbury. Ebook.

Kwei-Armah, Kwame (2007) *Statement of Regret.* London: Methuen Drama.

Kuti, Elizabeth (2006) *The Sugar Wife.* London: Nick Hern.

Levine, Philippa (2013) *The British Empire: Sunrise to Sunset*. Second edition. Abingdon: Routledge.

Loomba, Ania (2015) *Colonialism/Postcolonialism*. 3rd ed. Abingdon, UK: Routledge.

Luxemburg, Rosa (2003) *The Accumulation of Capital*. Abingdon: Routledge.

MacKenzie, John M. (1984) *Propaganda and Empire: The Manipulation of British Public Opinion, 1880–1960*. Manchester: Manchester University Press.

Marx, Karl (1995) *Capital: An Abridged Edition*. Oxford; New York: Oxford University Press.

Molefe, T.O. (2014) 'Racism and the Barbican's Exhibit B.' *New York Times*. 27 October 2014, date accessed 2 August 2015 <www.nytimes.com/2014/10/28/opinion/t-o-molefe-racism-and-the-barbicans-exhibit-b.html?_r=0>.

Moore, D.C. (2010) *The Empire*. London: Methuen Drama.

Nkrumah, Kwame (1968) *Neo-Colonialism: The Last Stage of Imperialism*. London: Heinemann.

Orr, Bridget (2001) *Empire on the English Stage 1660-1714*. Cambridge: Cambridge University Press.

Orwell, George (1984) 'Shooting an Elephant.' *The Penguin Essays of George Orwell*. Harmondsworth, UK: Penguin, 24–31.

Pagden, Anthony (2015) *The Burdens of Empire: 1539 to the Present*. Cambridge: Cambridge University Press.

Philips, Caryl, adapt. (2007) *Rough Crossings by Simon Schama*. London: Oberon.

Pilkington, Lionel (2010) *Theatre & Ireland*. Basingstoke: Palgrave Macmillan.

Pinnock, Winsome (2007) *A Hero's Welcome. Six Plays by Black and Asian Women Writers*. Ed. Kadija George. London: Aurora Metro.

Poore, Benjamin (2012) *Heritage, Nostalgia and Modern British Theatre: Staging the Victorians*. Basingstoke: Palgrave Macmillan.

Putnis, Peter (2010) 'News, Time and Imagined Community in Colonial Australia.' *Media History* 16:2, 153–70.

Ranger, Terence (1983) 'The Invention of Tradition in Colonial Africa.' *The Invention of Tradition*. Eds. Hobsbawm and Ranger, 211–62.

Rebellato, Dan (1999) *1956 and All That: The Making of Modern British Drama*. Abingdon, UK: Routledge.

Ritchie, Aileen (1999) *The Juju Girl*. London: Nick Hern.

Said, Edward W. (1994) *Culture and Imperialism*. London: Vintage.

Schumpeter, Joseph (1955) *Imperialism: Social Classes; Two Essays*. New York: Meridian.

Spivak, Gayatri Chakravorty (2010) 'Can the Subaltern Speak?' *Can the Subaltern Speak? Reflections on the History of an Idea*. Ed. Rosalind C. Morris. New York: Columbia University Press, 21–78.

Stanley, Henry Morton (1890) *Through the Dark Continent*. Sampson Low, Marston, Searle and Rivington. 2 vols.

Stockwell, Sarah (2008) 'Ends of Empire.' *The British Empire: Themes and Perspectives*. Ed. Sarah Stockwell. Oxford: Blackwell, 269–93.

Tidrick, Kathryn (2009) *Empire and the English Character: The Illusion of Authority*. London and New York: IB Tauris.

Tomlinson, John (1991) *Cultural Imperialism: A Critical Introduction*. London: Pinter.

Tucker Green, Debbie (2005) *Stoning Mary*. London: Nick Hern.

Vian, Boris (1971) *The Empire Builders*. London: Methuen.

Wertenbaker, Timberlake (1989) *Our Country's Good*. London: Methuen.

Wilkins, Alan (2007) *Carthage Must Be Destroyed*. London: Nick Hern.

index

acknowledgements

I would like to thank series editor Dan Rebellato for his continued support, and for his inspiring example of how to think and write about theatre. The University of York funded the period of research that enabled me to work on the book. Thanks to my MA dissertation supervisor, Helen Gilbert, and the staff and my fellow research students in the Department of Drama and Theatre at Royal Holloway University of London, who commented on parts of this project when it was in its earliest stages.

This book is for Kelly and Lydia.